Ash hoisted himself out of the pool in one powerful action, picked up a towel from a lounger and wrapped it around his waist.

"Going to roll the dice, Merle?"

He knew already. But now *he* waited. Yet by just being near such a source of outrageous vitality, she finally felt emboldened and empowered enough to step from the shadows and speak up.

"I've decided I want..." She broke off, battling the furious blush she felt swamping her skin.

He stood more still than she was. "Want?"

She breathed out. This still wasn't easy. "What you dared. You. Here. Now."

Ash's customary wicked smile didn't light up his face. Instead, he continued to look alarmingly serious. "You said you never overindulge and you ran away the second I offered dessert."

She had. She'd turned tail and fled, overwhelmed by the thoughts in her own damned mind. "You said I don't indulge at all. You were right."

His gaze locked on her more intently.

"I want to finish what we started in the bunker." Merle's wish slipped out. "In fact, I want more."

Rebels, Brothers, Billionaires

Reputation precedes them, temptation will redeem them.

Playboy Ash and hard-edged Leo Castle are just two of their philandering father's heirs. Which means they've inherited much more than a huge fortune and luxury property portfolio. Their father's notoriety follows them wherever they go…

Determined to step out of the shadow of scandal, the half brothers strive to defy expectation at every turn. Until rebellion comes up against desire so strong it's halted in its tracks!

Discover Ash's story in
Stranded for One Scandalous Week
Available now!

And look out for Leo's story
Coming soon!

Natalie Anderson

STRANDED FOR ONE
SCANDALOUS WEEK

HARLEQUIN
PRESENTS

ISBN-13: 978-1-335-40412-1

Stranded for One Scandalous Week

Copyright © 2021 by Natalie Anderson

This edition published by arrangement with Harlequin Books S.A.

For questions and comments about the quality of this book, please contact us at CustomerService@Harlequin.com.

Harlequin Enterprises ULC
22 Adelaide St. West, 40th Floor
Toronto, Ontario M5H 4E3, Canada
www.Harlequin.com

Printed in U.S.A.

USA TODAY bestselling author **Natalie Anderson** writes emotional contemporary romance full of sparkling banter, sizzling heat and uplifting endings—perfect for readers who love to escape with empowered heroines and arrogant alphas who are too sexy for their own good. When she's not writing, you'll find Natalie wrangling her four children, three cats, two goldfish and one dog... and snuggled in a heap on the sofa with her husband at the end of the day. Follow her at natalie-anderson.com.

Books by Natalie Anderson

Harlequin Presents

The King's Captive Virgin
Awakening His Innocent Cinderella
Pregnant by the Commanding Greek
The Greek's One-Night Heir
Secrets Made in Paradise

Conveniently Wed!
The Innocent's Emergency Wedding

Once Upon a Temptation
Shy Queen in the Royal Spotlight

The Christmas Princess Swap
The Queen's Impossible Boss

Visit the Author Profile page
at Harlequin.com for more titles.

For Heather—thank you always for your support and cheer. I hope you enjoy this one, too!

CHAPTER ONE

MERLE JORDAN WAS surrounded by bubbles. White frothy ones filled the deep, wide bath, petite ones fizzed from the oversized champagne bottle she'd just opened, while the fragile glass bubbles of a sleek modern light fixture gleamed above her head. The glimmering orbs delighted her starved senses, bringing absolute bliss.

She opened the stunning glass doors which led to the balcony that stretched the length of the building and ended with a curling staircase that led down to the pool below. A massive moon hung in the sky like the biggest bubble of all, casting a rippling sweep of light across the private bay. Merle lit the candle beside the bath and switched off the pretty light overhead, indulging in the soft, muted glow of the large moon and small flame.

With a disbelieving giggle she wriggled out of her underwear. She'd barely sampled the champagne but this decadence wasn't something she'd experienced and it was heady. Merle didn't excel at self-care at the best of times and this was beyond beginner level. She'd gradu-ated to expert in one go. Never before had she been in a bath so big, never had she seen a view so stunning, never had she stood naked and sipped champagne from a slender crystal glass. Never had she stolen time for herself.

The summer air was still warm but she couldn't resist the bubbles of the bath a moment longer. The glistening suds slipped over her like soft strokes of indulgence. Sliding deeper, Merle sipped her drink and breathed in the magnificent surroundings. She couldn't believe she was living in this 'holiday home'. She could bathe like this every night for the next six weeks if she wished.

It wasn't really a holiday home, it was a mega-mansion on Waiheke—an island less than an hour from Auckland, the largest city in New Zealand. Known as a playground for the wealthy, this property was a perfect example of the luxury homes hidden here. Incredibly private, it overlooked a beach with boat-only access and was furnished with an overflowing wine cellar, stunning swimming pool and spa. There was also a home gym, a cinema room, and even a single-lane bowling alley. The entire property was beautifully decorated with simple yet luxurious style. Richly coloured timber floors provided warmth and white paintwork offered crisp freshness, while soft-cushioned sofas and artfully placed occasional chairs invited relaxation. The gorgeous glazing of the house meant the entire building could be opened up to invite the outside in, and baskets with verdant plants accentuated that coastal, nature-loving style.

The place was ready for a magazine shoot at a moment's notice, Merle mused. Unusually for her, she liked the dearth of personal items in the decor; it made her feel it was more of a holiday venue and less as if she was encroaching on someone's private space. Besides, all those personal secrets were waiting to be discovered in the boxes currently filling the triple-car garage. She'd been contracted to sort and list their contents and prepare them either for storage or destruction.

She couldn't believe that such a property had sat unoccupied for over a year. It seemed wrong when so many people didn't have a home—including her. But she could hardly resent the obscenely wealthy owner's abandonment, given that the live-in requirement of the job gave her a roof over her head for a while. And, as it was Friday night, she'd decided it was okay to finally relax. Everyone deserved a treat after a hard week's work, right?

Sighing with pure, luxurious pleasure, she knelt up to replenish her champagne from the bottle she'd left on the ledge.

'Oh, hey, darling.'

The low, lazy murmur shocked her.

'Why are you naked in my bath?' he asked.

Half kneeling out of the bubbles, her hand stretched towards that champagne bottle, Merle froze, gaping at the man leaning against the doorjamb. For a second she only saw his eyes. They gleamed in the candlelight with an amber, almost animal warmth that didn't just dazzle, but actually stunned a woman into stillness.

Ashton Castle.

Merle breathed out, relieved because she'd instantly recognised him. He was in a photo downstairs, the one personal item on display in the place. He'd inherited this house when his father, Hugh, had died just over a year ago, but had ignored it since. Ash had been too busy to be bothered, right? He had his hands too full with every socialite or model or influencer who crossed his path. And they all said yes because not only was notorious playboy Ash Castle eye-wateringly rich, he was also appallingly good-looking.

Confronted by the reality, not a decades-old photo, Merle was stupefied. Tall, dazzling, *devastating*. She stared slack-jawed and wide-eyed at his long, muscular lines and stunningly sculpted face. She knew he also had that other irresistible-to-many facet to his nature—he was reckless. That was catnip to lots of women, wasn't it? They wanted to dance with danger, attempt to tame the untameable, bring the rich, ravishing, reckless playboy to heel…

But not Merle. She couldn't think of a worse combination.

She was sure his money, privilege and good looks meant it was too easy for him to get everything and everyone he wanted. That led to lazy arrogance and entitlement that meant the usual boundaries were ignored. She knew those sorts of men well. She'd been burned by one in her youth and she'd successfully avoided all of them since. Until now, when she was confronted with the worst of them all.

'Sweetheart?' Ash's gaze narrowed slightly.

Belatedly Merle realised she was up on her knees and, while there were masses of bubbles in the enormous bath, there weren't enough to cover her completely. Her breasts were exposed and quite possibly her…

She splashed down into the water so quickly she almost slipped right under. Desperately she threw her arms out to clutch the sides while drawing her knees up defensively at the same time. Another deep breath later, she wiped away the blob of frothy bubbles she could feel sliding down the side of her face.

Of all the people to have arrived unexpectedly. Of all the *times*. Of all the shocks.

And she couldn't stop staring. His dark grey tee hugged his broad shoulders and clung to the hard planes of his chest, while his black jeans emphasised the length and strength of his legs. They were faded in the thigh area, the paler patches drawing her eye to the core of his masculinity. She snapped her gaze from his slim hips back up past his broad shoulders, but his face only added to that impression of absolute masculinity. The shadow on his jaw highlighted its sharp, angular line. Beneath his straight nose, his sensually full lips curved into a weary but appreciative smile. And then there were those mesmerising eyes—a warm brown with an almost leonine hint in the amber. Everything about him screamed virile male. And the truly horrific thing was that her body—her weak, treacherous body—seemed to want nothing more than to melt in a purely sexual reaction. It was a primal, utterly basic response that was so new, so surprising, she couldn't pull her scattered thoughts together enough to scream at him to get out of there.

'Why are you here?' he asked negligently, still leaning against the doorjamb, apparently unfazed by her nudity and her panicked slide back into the water.

Of course he wasn't bothered. He was well used to women baring all around him.

Merle burned, mortified. That should be *her* question. But she wasn't great at speaking up, even when necessary. The truth was Leo Castle—Ash's half-brother and the man who'd confirmed her contract here—had said she'd have the place to herself, that she could take six weeks or more on the project if necessary. The prospect of having a home for that long had been incredible. She desperately needed to recover her affairs. She had no regrets about going into debt for her grandfather's health, but now that he was gone she had to claw her way out of the deep financial hole she'd been left in.

'Did someone send you, Miss…?'

Merle stiffened, perceiving slight insolence in his tone and finally found her voice. 'Leo Castle—'

'Leo hired you?' Ashton Castle's eyebrows rose, as if he was surprised. 'How did he know I was coming?' He looked perplexed as he muttered, apparently to himself, 'But he knows I don't do prostitutes.'

Merle sat stupefied all over again, suddenly unable to feel whether the water was hot or cold because everything had gone numb. Had he just said *prostitutes*?

Her heart pounded. Did he think she'd been hired to *entertain* him? That she was waiting naked in this bath with this champagne, ready to…to *please* him? A humiliation bomb exploded—bursting every one of her happy bubbles that'd been fizzing only five minutes before. And then a cloud of something else rose inside—something sinful and hot and that she couldn't bear to define.

'I think there's been a mistake,' she choked, so awash with embarrassment she was unable to continue.

'Yeah.' He strolled nearer and picked up the bottle of champagne from the edge of the bath, studying her even more closely, more *directly*—an open, unashamedly sexual appraisal. 'But worse ones have been made.'

With a twist of his full lips he cocked his head and cast that searing glance over the champagne label. '*This* was not a mistake, however. This was a nice choice.' He glanced back at her, laughter glinting in his eyes. 'At nine hundred dollars a bottle, you're not afraid to set your value high.'

What? Merle nearly choked again.

'It cost how much?' Her voice faded in a welter of shyness.

Ash smiled and Merle just about died. The transformation from serious sex god, to *smiling* sex god made every muscle inside her squeeze. She could only stare— yet again rendered stupid. He met her gaze square on. But as her brain slowly came back online she registered a tired edge in his eyes that meant that his smile didn't quite ring true. Drawing in a deep breath, she dragged her gaze back to the bottle and regretted ever thinking it was okay to accept the offer to have anything she wanted from the cellar.

'I had no idea. I'm sorry,' she mumbled, even more mortified. *Nine hundred dollars?* It was incredible to her that a bottle of anything could possibly cost that much. 'Mr Castle said I could—'

'Look, sweetheart, you fill your bath with it for all I care,' Ash interrupted her embarrassed explanation with an almost dismissive boredom. 'Bathe in every last drop if you want.'

But then his gaze skimmed across her shoulders and something else gleamed again.

She had the scandalous sensation that he was envisaging licking the droplets from her skin. And she *wanted* him to. Merle—who'd never wanted any man near her—suddenly wanted the biggest playboy of all to do what he wanted with his tongue and her skin, and how was it possible that she was slithering beneath some wordless spell?

Instinctively sinking lower into the water, Merle felt that awful softening deep inside. It was shockingly inappropriate, and she was appalled by herself as much as she was by him. Merle didn't feel hot and bothered by *anyone*. Yet she was unable to tear her gaze away from Ash Castle. It was as if she'd met a mythological creature—something rare and impossible. People simply didn't look like this in real life. Not with glinting strength and sinfully arching dark eyebrows and casually tousled, slightly too long hair that fell just so. Not with sharply defined jawlines, even when masked by the stubble of a long day, not with full, sensual mouths that curved upwards in invitation even when in repose.

But now his expression clouded as he gazed back at her. As she watched—too flummoxed to be able to do anything else—a heated heaviness filled the atmosphere between them. Neither of them moved. Merle didn't even breathe as his expression intensified. If she weren't already going crazy, she'd think he was as captivated by her as she was him.

'Do you like the taste?' he muttered. 'Because I like the look. Very much.'

She simply couldn't reply.

'And I must be tired,' he muttered as he lifted the champagne and took a long swig straight from the over-priced bottle, his hot gaze not leaving her face. 'I'm so tempted—'

'I've been hired by Mr Castle to sort out your father's collections,' Merle blurted quickly, knowing her cheeks were blazing with a dreadful blush.

Ash stilled for a second, then slowly set the bottle back down on the side of the bath. 'Pardon?'

She didn't believe the laziness in his tone, not when she saw the lethal alertness that had sprung into his eyes.

'Mr Leo Castle hired me to sort out your father's things,' Merle mumbled miserably, barely able to inject volume into her voice and utterly unable to hold his gaze. 'I'm an archivist. I've been staying here since Wednesday. I'm working on the papers in the boxes first.'

'An archivist?'

She hesitated, taking in a breath to summon the equilibrium to explain further. She hadn't spoken this much in days. 'Aside from the rare books, there are several dozen boxes stacked in the garage. I'm also cataloguing the art and the wine collections, though expert valuers will deal with those once I've done the detailed lists. I'm only doing the storage and destruction plan for the papers.' She paused for breath and glanced up to find he wasn't really listening to her explanation anyway.

'That's why you're in my bath?'

'I didn't know it was your bath,' she said. 'I didn't want to use the main bedroom. I thought this was one of the guest rooms.'

Something flickered in his expression before he shut it back to bland. 'I guess in recent years that is what it has been. But a long time ago it was my room.' He stared at her a little longer. 'I feel surprisingly disappointed.'

Her jaw dropped. She ought to be outraged, but the awful thing was she actually felt a touch flattered. Maybe the champagne had already had more of an effect on her than she'd realised?

'How long are you here for?' His forehead wrinkled.

She had to swallow before she could answer. 'Six weeks. But it might run a little longer as there's more than was initially listed…'

He lifted one of the large, fluffy white towels from the rack and placed it beside the champagne bottle. 'I didn't realise Leo had got that underway.'

'Mr Castle seemed to think the place would be empty for the duration of my contract.'

'Ordinarily he would've been right.' Ash's mouth tightened. 'Maybe it's best if we continue this conversation downstairs. Ten minutes, okay?'

She stared at him, shocked. Wasn't he going to apologise for thinking she'd been hired as his evening's entertainment?

He stared back at her, his head tilting as he read her expression, and that wicked smile flashed again, banishing what had barely been a hint of remorse. 'Unless you're happy to negotiate terms in here…?'

'Of course not,' she mumbled.

'Don't be embarrassed. I'm not.' He seemed amused by the colour she knew was climbing her cheeks again. 'Sex work is legal in this country.'

'I'm aware, but it's not my chosen profession.' She wanted to slide right under the bubbles, she really did.

He shrugged carelessly. 'Can you blame me for the mistake? The scene was perfectly set—candles, champagne, and you were beautifully positioned to maximise the effect of your…assets.'

His gaze didn't waver from hers—didn't drop to assess those 'assets' once more. And right now, those assets felt tight and achy and it was appalling.

'It's not unusual for you to find a woman just waiting for you in your bath or bed?' she asked huskily, shocking herself with the question. She never talked to anyone about such things.

'Not unusual in the least.' He grinned, the devilish lights in his eyes twinkling. 'It's something I enjoy. A lot.'

But he didn't pay them to be there. They arrived by choice—because of *want*.

Merle glared at him, horrified by her own reaction, her own wild thoughts. Since when did she feel anything thing like attraction to someone so…so…*smugly* sexual?

'Pleasure is something to be valued and appreciated,' he added almost piously. 'Not embarrassed about.'

And, with that pithy piece of sexual arrogance, he left.

Merle waited, almost completely submerged, until he'd vanished. The second he closed the door she scrambled out of the slippery bath. She dressed quickly in loose jeans and a tee shirt and threw on a baggy sweatshirt for good measure, despite still burning from that mortifying moment. She left her hair in its damp twist on top of her head and checked her reflection. For a millisecond she stared at her make-up-free skin and wished she was something she wasn't.

Fool. Why suddenly think of mascara and lipstick? She did *not* want his interest. Judging by the pictures she'd seen in the media, she wasn't anything like the women he usually met and that was a good thing. And, while she'd like a boyfriend one day, Ash Castle wasn't ever anyone's *boyfriend.* He was a lover, a seducer, an unrepentant playboy who doubtless left a mountain of broken hearts behind him. Merle's wasn't going to be one of them. As if he'd ever be interested anyway. It was only *context* that had made that glint flash in his face for those few seconds. She shrank in embarrassment, refusing to think about what he may or may not have seen of her in that bath. Or what he'd have thought.

'Are you usually based on Waiheke or in Auckland?' Ash called from where he stood in the centre of the atrium the second she appeared on the staircase. 'Because it's late. I'm not sure how we'll get you back to Auckland now the last ferry has already left.'

Merle descended slowly, stopping three steps from the bottom so she could keep her distance yet be able to look him directly in the eyes. She couldn't leave here. Not tonight or any other night for the next six weeks.

'I came here to do some work. I need space and peace,' he added when she didn't reply, and his gaze grew pointed.

'You'll have that,' she muttered, hoping to assure him despite the sudden racing of her pulse. 'You won't even know I'm here.'

His mouth tightened, then curved into a slow, deliberate smile that yet again didn't quite reach his eyes.

'Won't I? When you're naked in my bath and sleeping in my bed?'

She stared, sure he'd worded that deliberately to put those inappropriate images in her mind and unsettle her all over again. 'I'll switch to another room, of course.'

She tried to breathe away the blush she felt beating across her face and trained her own gaze a little lower. It wasn't the wisest move. He had the most perfect cheekbones; they were like blades, angling towards the arrogant set of his chin and his full mouth. And she really shouldn't look at his mouth. The full sensuality of it made her think of hunger and kisses. She forced her focus back up to his eyes. They were intent upon her, but within their heated gaze there was more than unhappiness growing. There was misery. *Why?*

'Delay your work for a week,' he said abruptly. 'Head home for a holiday. Full pay, of course.'

She instantly forgot her curiosity. Head home? To *where* exactly? She stared, unable to think of a reply as her anger built. Why did he need this enormous house all to himself? Why this one, when he had all those others? Aside from being a whizzy finance billionaire in his own right, she knew he was the heir to the Castle Holdings luxury apartment empire in Australia. His father had amassed a huge amount of property over there—where Ash Castle was supposed to be living right now.

But the man standing before her was obviously used to getting everything his way. To 'full paying' away any annoying inconveniences. And, not so deep beneath her surface, she smarted from the sting of his rejection. It was stupid, especially given the fact that she was well used to rejection.

For once in his life Ash Castle wasn't getting everything he wanted. At least, not tonight. He'd arrived on a whim and it was too bad for him that she was already here—under contract and with nowhere else to go.

'I don't need a holiday,' she said stiffly. 'I need to do my job. Which means I need to stay here.'

'Until tomorrow.' He nodded. 'Then you can go home for a week.'

She gritted her teeth. 'Unfortunately, I'm between residences at present.' She hated having to inform him of the deeply personal fact.

'Between residences?' he echoed bluntly, his gaze sharpening. 'You mean you're homeless?'

She tensed even more. 'As I spend my time going from contract to contract, I've no need to set up a permanent residence.'

It was a lie. Very few jobs were live-in and the only reason she'd got this contract was because she'd been able to leap on a plane at short notice. Sonja, the manager of the archival company she worked for, had been going to do it but her early pregnancy had been reassessed as high risk and she'd asked Merle to step in at the last minute.

Unsurprisingly, Ash Castle stared disbelievingly, making her feel as if yet more mortifying explanation was necessary. She'd spoken more in the last five minutes than she had all week and her voice was still rusty.

'Archivists don't get paid incredibly well,' she muttered.

'You amaze me.' That untamed gleam glinted in his eyes and his lips twitched.

An odd little fire in her ignited. There was no need for him to be facetious.

'Plenty of incredibly important jobs are low-paid.' Her heart thudded at her daring. Merle didn't stand up to anyone. Certainly not a man like this. Her grandmother would've torn strips off her if she'd seen her even look at him.

'Is archival work incredibly important? I wasn't aware.'

She had the feeling there were a lot of important things he was unaware of.

He was watching her closely and his sudden smile was both irreverent and tantalising. 'Do you think there are things you can teach me?'

With that soft-spoken drawl he revealed himself completely. Jaded. Experienced. Cynical. Incorrigible. Everything she wasn't. But yes, she could teach him some things. Manners, for a start.

'It's not my job to teach you anything,' she said with a bravery she was far from feeling. 'You're a grown man and I'm sure you'll be able to figure things out for yourself. Eventually.'

For the merest moment Merle basked while he stared at her, his mouth slightly ajar. She ought to be cautious, as if she'd just prodded a sleeping dragon, yet she was strangely exhilarated.

'If you're prepared to delay the completion of the archival process and pay for me to stay in a nearby hotel and holiday for the week, while on full pay,' she said warily, feeling a wholly foreign confidence trickle in her veins, 'then of course I'll do as you wish and leave first thing in the morning. However, it's a weekend in the height of summer and this is a small, popular island with not that many accommodation options. Do you think you'll find me a place?'

He stared at her for a long second. His mouth compressed. 'You want *me* to find you a place?'

'*You* want me to leave.' She couldn't hold his gaze and found she needed to study the floor intently as that damned fire beat across her face. 'Alternatively, you could be the one to stay elsewhere.'

'What?' He sounded flummoxed.

A hitherto dormant imp of mischievousness took over her mouth. 'Would that put you out?' She darted a glance up at him and the rest spilled out softly. 'Are you not used to working for what you want?'

There was another moment in which he just stared at her. That unhappy emotion had vanished from his eyes, and there was only gleamingly sharp speculation now.

'Oh, I work hard to get what I want,' he said pointedly. 'And I always get it.'

How nice to be him. But as he held her gaze with a fierce intensity, Merle's bubble of bravado popped. Breaking into a sweat at her temerity, she dropped her gaze and surreptitiously watched him pull a phone from his pocket. It was a latest release, squillion-dollar tech toy. Of course.

'It's late to be making calls.' She worried her lower lip, already regretting her runaway, rogue tongue moment. She should have stayed quiet. She couldn't afford to lose this job. 'I—'

'But not too late to check an online bookings app,' he interrupted before she could apologise.

Merle watched, partly glad because he didn't deserve her apology. As he tapped and swiped the screen over the course of the next six minutes, his frown deepened and his jawline hardened. Merle's heart raced as his expression turned positively rigid.

'You're going to have to stay,' he finally gritted.

Was it bad to relish the fact that the man couldn't get his way? Doubtless it was a rare occurrence for him. And a *very* rare victory for her. A thrill shivered through her. She'd stood up to him and she'd won.

'You stay in my old room. I'll take the master suite.' He squared his shoulders and his smile was bitter-edged. 'Might as well exorcise all the demons while I'm here.' He lifted his gaze to ensnare hers once more, his lips twisting in a mocking smile. 'You'll have to work extra hard now you know I'll be here watching you.'

Her sliver of success melted in the face of what could only be described as a...*promise*. A veiled, heated, *inappropriate* promise.

Her pulse thickened and she regretted his change of mind. Wouldn't it be better for her to be as *far* away from him as possible while he was here? What had she been *thinking*? She'd wanted to win one over on him— the kind of guy who got everything his way all of the time. 'I thought you wanted space.'

She hadn't meant to say anything more but somehow it slipped out.

He regarded her beneath half-lowered lids. Merle found she was unable to move beneath the intensity of his gaze. Was this how he did it? Seduction by a simple stare?

'I thought I did,' he murmured. 'But I also enjoy watching interesting things, Miss...'

He didn't know her name. He'd made all kinds of assumptions and he didn't even know her name.

'Merle Jordan,' she said stiffly. And she wasn't 'interesting'.

'I'm Ash Castle.' He mock-bowed. 'But you already knew that.'

She nodded. It had been his arrogant, own-it-all air that had given him away but she awkwardly offered a more polite explanation. 'Your photo's in the study.'

A young Ash with his parents, captured on the beach just outside. His eyes widened, exposing a flash of that other emotion before his expression shuttered again.

Inside, she was feverishly panicked about getting through this. She'd avoid him entirely for the next week. Fortunately, she was well used to staying out of sight and silent. All those years of hiding like a mouse in the wings of her mother's performances would finally come in handy. Not to mention hiding from her grandmother's shouting. It wouldn't be hard at all to avoid him in a house this size, plus she had all those boxes to bury herself in.

Yet, intriguingly, as he hesitated his expression turned more than serious, more than sombre, more akin to misery. It didn't suit him. A tinge within Merle tugged her down the stairs towards him.

'No one knows I'm here,' he said. 'Not even Leo. I'd like to keep it that way.'

'Of course,' she mumbled.

He didn't realise she had no one to tell and she was far removed from anyone in his world. But she did need to stay here. Not only did she have nowhere else to go, but this was also an important job for her professionally. She had debt to clear and a future to forge.

'You won't even know I'm here.' But as she earnestly attempted to reassure him, she saw the look in his eyes morph once more.

CHAPTER TWO

YOU WON'T EVEN know I'm here.

Well, *that* was impossible. Ash scowled. How was he going to forget the sight of her gleaming in the moonlight like a welcome beacon? She'd been rising out of that bath like a dryad at a magical spring, complete with champagne fountain and a flushing allure that had transfixed him. Only he'd been so jaded he'd mistaken her for a woman of the night and said so. Even for him it had been inappropriate, an unthinking utterance of the first possibility his tired brain had come up with. *Wishful* thinking, if he was being completely honest. The fantasy of her waiting nymph-like to give him pleasure had made perfect, albeit impossible, sense. He should've held his outrageous, rebellious tongue, but he never yet had.

And now?

He *needed* to be alone, but he'd never been going to stay a full week. It was going to be a couple of days max. He'd just wanted her well out of the way so he could be clear of any human contact while he absorbed the shock of what had been done to the place. But now he was stuck with her. Yet he wasn't feeling as irritated about that as he had been only a second ago.

Yesterday's headline should've been easy to ignore. The newspaper article comparing 'playboy rebel Ash' to his illegitimate half-brother, Leo, the 'responsible leader', had been rubbish. Yet it had forced him into the action he'd been deferring for months. Almost a year ago, Ash had inherited everything. His father, Hugh Castle, had refused to recognise Leo right to the end. He'd also refused to believe Ash's own refusal to be involved in the family business. No matter that they'd been estranged for a full decade and that Ash hadn't once set foot inside the company headquarters or any of the family properties in all that time. Or that he'd deliberately set out to make his own fortune—taking risks purely to have the satisfaction of being more successful to spite his father.

None of that had mattered. His father, as always, didn't listen, didn't care and only did what *he* wanted. As Ash was Hugh's first-born, legitimate male heir, it was onto his unwilling shoulders that the company had been foisted. But Ash had immediately moved to ensure *all* Hugh Castle's heirs got their fair share. He'd intended to liquidate all assets and split the wealth. But Leo had asked for a different solution. It wasn't that Ash had 'abandoned responsibility', *forcing* Leo to take over Hugh's company, Leo had insisted. He'd been determined to take over. Ash had simply stood aside and let him. How could he say no when Leo had been denied so much by the Castle family already?

Ash had half expected his half-brother to raze Castle Holdings to the ground. He wouldn't have blamed him, in fact he would've enjoyed watching. But Leo hadn't done that. Leo had obviously inherited integrity from his mother. Maybe growing up away from the malignant force that had been their father had benefited him.

Whereas Ash was utterly his father's son. Careless. Ruthless. Selfish.

But there was one particular problem Ash *had* been avoiding. This last personal property—the former family holiday home on Waiheke Island. The press would never think to look for him here. No one would, which was why he should've realised the idea of Leo arranging a woman for him was ridiculous. It wasn't in his ultra-responsible half-brother's playbook. Truthfully, it wasn't in his either. And this woman was no courtesan. She couldn't underline that fact more boldly than with the monstrously oversized clothes she'd hurriedly thrown on. But the swamping swallow-her-whole trousers and sweatshirt were too late. Ash had seen her naked and one part of him had already made meticulously detailed plans for her very luscious body.

'The place is large enough for us to avoid each other completely,' Merle Jordan reiterated in that shy, low, sexy-as-sin voice.

Ash stared as the colour in her luminous skin increased and her beautiful brown eyes darkened. His gloom evaporated as his intuition purred. He had to suppress a satisfied smile.

She was *bothered*. It wasn't just because of what he'd said or done. The underlying cause was as obvious as it was reciprocated by him. Instant interest—the immediate recognition of physical, pleasurable, possibilities. Admittedly, they were possibilities she seemed determined to reject. Yet *she* was the one who'd insisted on staying here. Who'd insisted he discover for himself how impossible it was to find other accommodation on the island. Who'd wanted to teach him a lesson. It had actually pleased him to learn that he'd be able to sell even this ultra-expensive property quickly and easily, given the popularity of all pricing levels of accommodation. So her plan hadn't only backfired, it'd also had a beneficial consequence.

'Don't you think?' she added.

Maybe there could be more than one benefit. But then he saw the anxiety lurking in the backs of those beautiful eyes.

She's bothered because she's worried about being homeless, you idiot.

At his silence that blush swamped her face again. She'd almost stammered as she'd pushed past her shyness to fight for her place here. It had cost her to admit to him the truth of her circumstances. The confession hadn't been an attempt at manipulation, but rather dragged out of her in raw embarrassment. It drew a response from deep within him too. The feeling shimmered again now and reminded him of another woman who'd also been alone and vulnerable and awkwardly shy. One who he'd stepped forward to help. But back then the flare of protectiveness within Ash had ended in a destructive mess.

Back. Away.

He should leave. Yet the temptation to do the absolute opposite almost overwhelmed him. He wanted to reach out and slide his fingertips down her neck, to push aside that baggy sweatshirt and explore her skin, to draw her close and kiss her past comfortable and right on to pleasured. The concentration required to stop himself made him ache. This chemistry at first sight was explosive. For all of his success with women, it *wasn't* something he was used to. He played around but never foolishly. Now it was as if a fever had taken hold. He forced his gaze beyond her, focusing on the house to pull himself together.

It was exactly the shock he needed.

The beach house had always stolen his breath—one moonlit glimpse of the inky water was enough to invoke that old sense of freedom. But the house itself had been altered beyond recognition—entire walls were gone, replaced with larger, newer elements. He'd yet to see all the renovations, but what he could see was so changed. That first feeling of freedom was strangled in seconds by anger. Regret. Self-recrimination. The last time he'd been here was the last time he'd seen his mother alive. And he'd disappointed her so badly.

He refused to remember. But he'd been refusing to remember for a long time now. And after yesterday's article?

The piece had celebrated his 'sainted' father before speculating and comparing his disparate sons' lives yet again. Ash still couldn't fathom how his father had been held in such high esteem for so long. Even after Ash had exposed Hugh Castle's cheating soul to the world by providing Leo with a DNA sample to prove he was Hugh's illegitimate son, his old man's other successes had overridden any punishment he should have faced. Hugh had been miraculously forgiven not just by his beloved 'society circles', but by the media and court of public opinion too. Even though the lying old jerk had spent years denying Leo's birthright, years destroying Leo's mother's reputation.

Who could blame Hugh for a few transgressions when he'd suffered the heartbreak of a dying wife for so long?

As though his father were the victim. Empathetic explanations were offered and forgiveness assured. But not by Ash. Never by him. The falsity of it all was something he couldn't forget. Indeed, the abbreviation of his name was apt. Because all Ash could offer were the acrid, smoking remnants of what had once been. And all he wanted to do was destroy what was left of his father's legacy. For him this place on Waiheke Island was the core—the most obvious construct of his father's deceit. It was the ultimate symbol of his father's ability to build over the truth with nothing but a fabrication of perfection.

That article had forced all those feelings up and he'd finally come to face the poisonous betrayal of his father's last actions. To say his final, bitter goodbye so he could forget it all for ever. To finish it, so Leo didn't need to trouble. But his capable half-brother had already stepped in. He'd hired Merle Jordan to sort out the vast personal collections that had been dumped here in the aftermath of their father's death. Was there any need for Ash to stay here at all?

Bitterness and an acrid sense of futility swamped him—scouring off the old scab and exposing the raw wound he'd been hiding for years. He'd been helpless the last time he was here, too—watching his desperately unwell mother. Disappointing her beyond redemption. But there *was* one last thing he needed to do for her—

despite his inability to ever secure her forgiveness. And that task wasn't right for a stranger's hands—not even the soft, light, careful hands of the archivist standing before him. It was a job only for Ash. He couldn't avoid it any longer. He had enough regrets regarding his mum already. So he had to stay for a day or so at least to accomplish this last for her—he'd go through her things and dispose of them himself.

Like most people, Ash infinitely preferred pleasure to pain. And the memories he couldn't restrain now were the worst of his life. So what else could he do but glance again at the welcome radiance of his initially unwanted housemate?

The luscious Merle Jordan's hair was still mostly tied up in that messy pile while a few wispy curls lingered from the damp heat of the bath. She wore not an ounce of make-up but her pouty lips were a tantalising pink and her eyes were like dark pools in secret caves—their depth indeterminable, possibly dangerous, but still so damn inviting. His senses begged him to step closer, to stare deeper, to touch and discover if she was as soft and yielding as she looked. Sex had always been an escape and he needed escape more than anything in this bitterest of returns.

'I'm hungry, Merle.' He couldn't resist voicing his thoughts.

Her eyes widened and he could've sworn the pulse at the base of her neck fluttered faster.

'Is there anything delicious to eat?' he added lazily, unable to resist the pleasure of watching her react to such a very little tease.

She swallowed. 'Um…'

'Or do I have to find that out for myself as well?'

He suppressed the smirk at her visible flare of irritation.

'There's…' Her voice faded away.

'Not much?' he gathered drily, wondering how much more it would take to provoke the real response he just knew she was thinking.

Her expression turned mutinous. Her lashes fluttering her eyes a direct stare into his pitiful soul.

'Didn't you bring anything with you?'

He smiled. It was the slightest of stands with a hint of scorn. She thought he was spoiled and, yes, that was exactly what he was. He'd make no apologies for it or for any of his other faults. But he liked that tiny glimpse of her spirit. He wanted to see more of it. More of her—all over.

Frankly, he didn't expect to have *all kinds* of appetites roused here and now.

But as he gazed at her, suffering her wide-eyed scrutiny, something else tugged inside him. A very small desire to do a little better. He abruptly turned and stalked to the kitchen. But he was keenly aware of her following him with that intriguingly subversive look barely hidden in her expression.

Once there, he scoped the shelves, but there were limited signs of her presence. In the fridge there was a single block of cheese. On one shelf in the pantry there were a few small tins of fish, a couple of packets of instant noodles and a box of crackers. Just looking at her pathetic supplies made his stomach rumble.

'What do you exist on?' he grumbled, glancing over to where she stood on the other side of the large kitchen counter, primly holding her hands together and pursing her very kissable lips.

'I have sufficient supplies.'

'Sufficient?' he echoed drily. 'How sad. Why have merely sufficient when you can have *satisfying*?'

Colour tinged her cheeks again. He couldn't resist acting up the outrageousness he knew she expected from him. She thought he was an irresponsible play-boy? He was quite happy to perform if it meant he kept seeing her blush.

'Instant noodles.' He groaned. They weren't even decent flavours.

'They're delicious.'

'I prefer my noodles hand-pulled and fresh.' He knew he sounded awful, but it was too much to keep from pulling another eye-roll from her. He poked through the tins and came across a small stack of individual steamed puddings—complete with caramel sauce. They were little single-serve tubs to go in the microwave.

'Oh, here we go.' He glanced at her slyly. 'So you're not afraid to spoil yourself in secret?'

Of course she wasn't. Hadn't he just caught her in-dulging in a luxurious candle-lit bubble bath while sipping over-priced champagne? She had a decadent, sensual streak.

She stared at him, those eyes widened in shock. Then he saw her chin tilt.

'You want to eat my little dessert?' Her voice was impossibly breathy.

No. He wanted to eat her. And they both knew it. He stared at her, stilled by the glimpse of steel in her eyes. And of heat.

'You think you can just swoop in and take what you want?' she added, despite the blush mottling not just her face but her neck too. 'No matter who it belongs to?'

Wasn't she a deliciously pointy creature when she let herself out?

'I'll always take what I want from someone who's willing to offer it to me,' he assured her.

He watched her warring with whether to speak again or not. He couldn't move, desperate for her to say it.

'I'm not offering anything,' she finally claimed.

'Not even one little bite of pudding?' he drawled. 'Damned if I'm going to spend the week living like I've been shipwrecked.'

She shouldn't settle for that either.

'You can't cope with a constraint on your appetite even for a little while?' she asked.

The little punch pleased him an inordinate amount.

'I don't like to be denied decent sustenance,' he answered lazily. 'I like delicious. It doesn't have to be a lot, but it does have to be quality.'

'A man like you will always want more than a morsel of perfection,' she said quietly. 'You wouldn't stop at one of those puddings, you'd want *all* of them.'

A morsel of perfection? He leaned against the bench and laughed. 'You think I have a voracious appetite?'

She slowly nodded, her baleful, brilliant gaze locked on him. 'Absolutely.'

'That's where you're wrong, my sweet,' he said lightly and then shot straight to the crux of the matter. 'I only ever have one bite. One night with a woman.'

She blinked. 'Only one night? Wow,' she muttered in that husky voice. 'That's too mean of you. Are you afraid she'll get bored if you let her stick around for longer?'

Ash regarded her steadily, masking the adrenalin and anticipation burgeoning inside. Merle Jordan had gone from a mortified, tongue-tied bundle of embarrassment, to a worthy opponent displaying claws and wit and he wanted to see so much more of it from her. 'I'm not afraid,' he countered softly. 'I'm merely protecting her from the inevitable heartbreak.'

'Oh, so it's *chivalry*,' she mock-marvelled, even as she dropped her gaze from his. 'How heroic of you to save her from yourself.'

'Quite,' he purred. She was an absolute, intriguing challenge. 'Now, Ms Jordan.' He held up one of the single-serve puddings. 'Are we going to label and lock away what's mine and label and lock away what's yours, or are we going to pool resources and share?'

At that, she gazed back up at him, despite her blushing breathiness. He could see the tremble in her fingers she was trying to hide and he respected the effort it took for her to hold his gaze. He willed her to say whatever pithy thing she was thinking. Because she was *definitely* thinking and he ached to know what about.

'Exactly what resources are *you* planning to bring to this party?' she finally asked.

Suddenly he had plans. Lots of very good, very pleasurable plans.

He'd thought he wanted to be alone to face this final goodbye and dispose of his mother's things. But perhaps, while he was here, alone was the one thing he *shouldn't* be. This disapproving woman might be the perfect antidote to take his mind off the mess of emotion this place conjured within. He *badly* needed distraction from the task he'd been dreading for almost a decade and here she was in bountiful, curvaceous perfection. Maybe he could tempt her out of her prickly shell? He could disarm her stand-offishness, break down her reserve…

If he got her to deign to talk to him? If he got her to laugh, that would be a bonus point for sure. And if she dined with him that would be a total win. He relished each possible challenge in a game he suddenly ached to play.

'Haven't you figured it out yet, Merle?' he teased, assuming full arrogance and amusement. 'I'll bring everything you could ever want.'

CHAPTER THREE

FIRST THING IN the morning, Merle had shut herself in the study with one of the many boxes from the stacks in the multi-car garage. While she wasn't contracted to work weekends, given the circumstances it seemed a good way of staying out of sight and out of trouble. The enormous wooden table in the cavernous room was perfect for sorting the mountain of papers and the work would occupy her completely for weeks.

Unfortunately, the floor-to-ceiling windows spanning the length of the study overlooked not just the gorgeous sea, but also the stunning infinity pool. And Ash Castle had been making the most of that pool for *hours*.

Last night he'd said he was here to work, but to Merle it didn't look as if he was doing anything other than hard-core exercising. He swam length after length. Every so often he emerged to perform push-ups and burpees on the beautifully landscaped deck. Given he was clad in nothing but black swim shorts, it was hard not to notice his lean, muscled strength. But it was his single-minded focus that fascinated her more. Intensely driven, he pushed himself like a man possessed.

Merle couldn't stop herself watching, equally impressed and aghast as he brought weights out from the gym and lined up the kettle bells into some sort of terrifying poolside circuit. He seemed determined to exhaust himself—which took a lot of effort because apparently the man was ultra-marathon-fit. Maybe the work he meant was some kind of one-week extreme make-over? Was he was going to be modelling or something? Or did he have some super-hot date next weekend that he wanted to be in peak shape for?

Merle couldn't think of anything worse.

Worse than that, she couldn't think of anything *else*. Ash Castle infuriatingly appeared in every thought— her sly mind kept replaying that mortifying moment when he'd walked in on her in his bath. And she kept seeing the wicked laughter in his eyes, the outrageousness in his tone…but the glimpse of tiredness and the fleeting depth of discomfort intrigued her even more. She suspected the man was more complicated than his superficial perfection presented. To make matters even worse she'd actually dreamt about him.

I'm hungry, Merle.

His frank admission had meant something else and her suddenly unreliable body had responded so inappropriately.

Everything you'd ever want.

She knew he meant sexually. And, as inexperienced as she was, she knew he *wasn't*. He'd deliver.

Annoyed with her basic instinct fixation, Merle pulled more papers from the box, determined to regain her customary indifference to men and the thought of sex in general. Men and Merle didn't mix. Ever. Actually, *people* and Merle rarely mixed. It wasn't surprising; she'd had an unusual childhood—hiding in the wings of her mother's shows, then suppressed by her strict disciplinarian grandmother who'd never really wanted her, then isolated at school, where her only escape had been hours at second-hand stalls with her quiet grandfather. She'd become even more isolated while caring for him. But now things were going to change and as soon as she'd got herself on a firm financial footing she'd feel braver about moving forward. Getting this job done would help immeasurably. Squaring her shoulders, she focused on the boxes. Ash Castle was a distraction she couldn't afford.

It turned out Hugh Castle had been old-school—keeping an extensive collection of everything from business files to correspondence, to orders of service from state functions, to menus from society weddings, to feature articles—mostly about himself. It wasn't surprising. The man had been massively successful. She labelled each item and inputted the details into the database she'd set up. But she still couldn't help thinking about his eldest son just outside. Reportedly, the cause of the division between Hugh and Ash had been Ash's wild lifestyle—all reckless partying and playboy rebellion. But Ash had forged his own success through high finance and venture capital—risky deals that had paid off. He had the gift.

Of course he did.

When Hugh died a year ago there'd been speculation regarding who'd inherit the vast estate—the wayward acknowledged son or the illegitimate son Hugh had refused to recognise. Ash had notoriously declined anything and everything to do with his father for years, yet even so it had stunned people to see Leo, the son Hugh had always denied, taking over the management of the flagship property company Castle Holdings.

Merle's own curiosity burgeoned, exacerbated by the physicality of the man outside the window. Why had Leo, not Ash, taken over? In a flash of weakness she typed his name into an online search engine—but it was the images that caught her attention. As she scrolled down the never-ending expanse of photos her stomach knotted. There were brunettes, blondes, redheads, women with long hair, bobs or elfin crops, thin and curvy and everything in between… The only thing they had in common was their smug, 'look at me' smiles. Merle sharply inhaled, staving off the acidic emotion. Surely she wasn't jealous?

Apparently Ash Castle had dated a huge, eclectic number of women over the last decade. Of course he had—wasn't it 'one night' only for him? Indeed, rarely did one woman feature in more than a few shots. Yet, while they all wore that satisfied smile, the look in *his* eyes didn't reflect the same. The gleam wasn't desire, more like resentment, and in many he'd raised his hand to block the blinding flash or push away the paparazzi blocking his path. The photos went back years, documenting a familiarity with a party lifestyle Merle hadn't experienced. She didn't want to. She liked her life as it was—*safe*.

She shut down the web browser. The pointless search hadn't assuaged her fascination. If anything, she was more curious. Ash didn't just operate in a different world, but a whole other stratosphere. She glanced again at the family photo on the mantlepiece in the study.

He stood between his parents in front of the beach. He looked about ten in the picture, but his eyes were unmistakable. Merle thought it interesting that, despite their estrangement, Hugh Castle had put this one personal picture pride of place in his holiday home.

She glanced out of the window and saw Ash swimming yet more lengths. Envy rippled over her. The afternoon heat had seeped into the study but she couldn't open the doors the way she had earlier in the week. Not with Ash only yards away and her determined to remain invisible. But it would have been nice to take a dip. Instead, she adjusted the air conditioning so it basically blasted ice at her.

Once she was finished here she'd sneak up to her suite for the evening. The room upstairs was opulent with a comfortable study area and balcony overlooking the pool and the bay, so she could hardly complain about being stuck in there. But she felt a pang of disappointment at the thought of the luxurious home cinema she'd spotted on her first day with its vast digital library. Tonight had been going to be her movie night— after Friday night's champagne bath pamper treat. She'd been looking forward to working out that fancy popcorn machine… Yet suddenly the fantasy scrolling through her head like some romance movie was of her curling up on that amazing lounge suite and watching a movie *with* Ash Castle…

Fool. That wouldn't be a romance, but a tragedy. Or, worse, a mockumentary. A prank plot line where the out-of-her-league girl thinks the perfect guy has become genuinely interested in her. It would end with her as the punchline. Again. She'd been humiliated by a perfect-looking popular guy once before and she wasn't up for a repeat. Those guys knew they were attractive, and they got it too easy, so they got bored and played games. Cruel ones. She knew, she'd been the target. So that fantasy bubble could just pop and disappear for good.

Besides, Ash Castle wasn't perfect. He was a play-boy. The type she'd been warned about all of her life by her super-strict grandmother—though truthfully, her grandmother had warned her about *all* men, and to be wary of her *own* desires. It was from her mother's experience that Merle knew the heat-of-the-moment temptation a man like Ash could inspire was nothing short of life-changing. That mistake wasn't one Merle was about to make. So, instead of the movie and the popcorn, she'd curl into that cosy armchair in her room with cheese and crackers. She'd celebrate surviving one whole day, and in a week he'd be gone.

Ash floated on his back and gazed up at the house through narrowed eyes, wondering if he'd actually imagined the whole woman-in-his-bath moment last night. Had she been some wishful mirage from his over-tired brain? A wistful fantasy of female perfection?

No. Not even *his* fertile mind could have conjured up such a stunning, ethereal yet earthy sample of feminin-ity, nor the horrors of her outfit afterwards. Now, the studied silence and stillness of the house irritated the hell out of him. Merle Jordan was the avoidance cham-pion of the world. He ought to *appreciate* that she was being quiet and staying out of sight, given he'd told her he'd come here for space when he'd tried to banish her from the premises.

Of course, peace was the last thing he could find. It was the first time he'd been back in years and memories tortured him. Echoes of old arguments rang in his head like faint wails of distant sirens, keeping him eternally on edge. That aim to sort his mother's things was impossible when he couldn't even bear to look around him. His father's redesign of the property was massive and so bitterly pointed. Every element of his mother's input had been erased. There wasn't just a new pool, but also a whole new guest wing with the private cinema and bowling alley, and the wine cellar had doubled in size. But it was the changes in his mother's beloved garden that had angered Ash to the point where he couldn't bear to walk beyond the pool area to see the full devastation. He'd tried to burn the fury out with a brutal workout, hoping to exhaust himself and finally silence his overthinking brain. It hadn't worked. He kept on thinking—though increasingly he kept thinking about *Merle*. She was an infinitely preferable subject.

Merle Jordan, mouse-like woman of mystery. What was she doing in there? How was she managing to stay so quiet? So out of sight? So deliberately invisible?

A fling wasn't what he was here for. And, despite the undeniable awareness flickering between them, she clearly didn't want it either. But of course, to Ash Castle and the contrary, spoiled mood he was in, that made her even more enticing. He liked a game and he liked to win. Isolation wasn't what he wanted any more. Not here, where the house that had once held such happiness had been so destroyed. Of course, it wasn't the renovations that had wrecked everything. That had been Ash himself. His own weakness was the culprit—the one he'd inherited from his cheating jerk of a father. He breathed in sharply and determinedly—blessedly— thought of Merle Jordan instead. She'd been mortified when he'd caught her naked in the candlelight but later she'd revealed a little sass. He wanted to see more of that—he was sure it was there. When she wasn't biting her tongue.

His skin tightened as he thought of her mouth. It was that fever again—he wished his extreme emotions would ease. Except, regarding Merle Jordan, they weren't really emotions. They were hormones. Sheer, mere, lust. But part of him welcomed the warmth of it. For all the partying, he'd been feeling cold these last few months. He'd attributed it to too much of the same game as always—long work hours, jaded social scene, easily won escapades. Boredom, in other words.

Merle Jordan wasn't boring. Merle Jordan wasn't like anyone he'd ever met. A very serious, homeless archivist.

By the late afternoon he was out of patience to wait any longer for when and how she might appear. He strode to the study, where he knew she'd set up her archival operation. He blinked as his eyes adjusted from the bright sunlight outside. He avoided looking at the cardboard box open on the floor, nor did he glance at the papers spread on the large table. He still wasn't ready.

Merle was standing by the table, a page in hand, staring at him, and he stared right back because *what* was she wearing? The white inspection gloves on her hands he could understand, but those coveralls? Akin to a hazmat suit, they enveloped her completely, only instead of white or blue or high-vis neon, they were all black. They were, without doubt, the most shapeless sack he'd ever seen.

'Is something wrong?' she asked nervously.

He could still only stare. Beyond the suit her skin was as luminous as he'd remembered and he lost himself in her dark brown eyes. They reminded him of rich chocolate, that sort he'd like to play with—to melt, then lick. As he watched, her eyes widened and grew darker. Velvet delicious. Her long brunette hair was held back in a loose braid that hung down her back. Utilitarian, yes. Also, stunning. He still couldn't stop staring.

'Mr Castle?'

That snapped him back to reality. 'Mr Castle' was his father, Hugh. He was Ash.

'How are you getting on?' he asked.

'Well, thank you.' Her polite response wasn't enough to sugar-coat her wish to dismiss him and only worsened his irritation. His own contrariness was killing him.

'Did you find a body in the bunker?' he muttered.

Her brown eyes widened fractionally before a flinch compressed her features. 'A…what?'

'A body. In the bunker,' he repeated unrepentantly and grinned as he gestured towards her. 'Hence the forensics fashion.'

He knew he'd been out of line, but he wanted her to unleash the spirit flaring in her eyes.

Her chin lifted. 'Very funny.'

Vitality flowed through his veins. It might be a frosty reaction, but he'd got her to speak.

'A lot of the boxes are dusty.' She iced her explanation with the coolest of tones. 'My "forensics fashion" protects my clothes.'

Even as fiery embarrassment stained her skin, the determined dignity in her restrained response made him squirm. To his amazement, Ash experienced a rare moment when he regretted his teen-acquired tendency to say whatever outrageous thing popped into his head. And what kind of sub-human was he for being annoyed that she was so well-covered by her clothing?

But as he watched, her smooth forehead wrinkled and her coolly assessing gaze narrowed. 'You were joking about a bunker, right?'

'You mean you don't know?' he drawled, as he realised an opportunity had suddenly opened up. She'd fallen for bait he'd not intended to set.

'If only you had a moustache, you could twirl the ends,' she muttered. 'Obviously I don't know, or I wouldn't have asked.'

He paused to savour the surprising sass of her answer. She was crisply to the point and her quietly crackling energy stoked his.

'There's a secret bunker,' he said, determined to snare her interest now.

'A relic from the war?' She frowned. 'Here on the property?'

'Sadly no, not a historic one. That would've been fascinating. This one is more…' *Bonkers*. He cleared his throat. 'It's new. My father had it installed.'

Her eyebrows lifted. 'You mean a panic room?'

'I think it's a little more over the top than that.' He'd not checked it out yet. He'd missed its construction entirely and had only become aware of its existence when

he'd read through the list of current contractors the estate was paying for. Because he'd been so out of sorts
at his glimpse of the garden, he'd avoided investigating
in full the other changes to the grounds. Having Merle
with him while he did might be a good diversion.

'Why would your father want a bunker?' She looked
confused. 'Why *here*?'

'Why indeed?' He had no idea, he just wanted to
avoid his history by focusing on her and he didn't want
her to disappear on him again yet. 'Want to see it?' he
purred.

Her eyes darkened even more, melting into delicious
pools of an unreadable emotion.

'I'm partway through this box,' she muttered.

It was a weak show of reluctance. An absurd level
of anticipation swept through him. Surely this was like
catnip to a woman who liked historical records and old
things?

'It'll still be here when we're done,' he replied easily,
trying not to let his eagerness for her company show
too obviously. 'Apparently, it's only in the garden. It
shouldn't take long.'

He watched, conscious of the increasing awareness
between them—the rising colour in her cheeks, the
thrum of heat in his blood.

'There might be all kinds of things stored in there
that should be considered for the archives,' he tempted.

'You don't know for certain?'

'I've not been in there yet.'

Surprise flashed. 'You've not yet ventured into a secret bunker that's been built here?'

He shook his head, suppressing the instinctive rejection of anything his father had built and focusing on her. 'Could be exciting, right?' he said blandly. 'Like discovering Tutankhamun's tomb?'

He watched as her mouth quivered, but she couldn't suppress her smile for long. A hard lump in his chest eased. One point on the board—he'd made her smile. And it had been worth the effort.

'Let me just finish up with this letter.' She put the document she held onto the table, drawing his attention to his father's things. Things that made his skin crawl. Things he wanted to burn.

'You don't wear glasses?' he asked, distraction a necessity as she marked up something with her pencil.

'Stereotype, much?' she muttered coolly. 'Bookish girl must need glasses?'

He laughed. *This* was what he'd needed, a little sparring with someone determined to remain uninterested. Except she already was. He *knew* she was. And that wasn't all arrogance. Sparks like this were never one-sided.

'Actually, I asked because of the lamp you're using. It casts an unusual light.'

'It's to avoid damaging the documents,' she explained as she added something else to the paper. 'It's not for my eyes. I have perfect eyesight.'

'Perfect?' he echoed with amusement. 'You can see right through me, huh?'

She glanced over and shot him an instant kill look. That heaviness in his chest thawed fractionally more. 'You already know I can.'

'Yet you've been avoiding me,' he said when she finally stepped away from the table.

'You came here to be alone,' she said, her expression devoid of the coy flirtatiousness that he was used to from women. 'I've been giving you the space you asked for.'

He'd been regretting that request since the moment he'd made it. Though, contrarily, he equally regretted not insisting that she leave. Truthfully *he* was the one who ought to leave. He shouldn't have come back. It had only dredged up memories he'd fought hard to forget. A reminder of who he was and the family failings he couldn't ever escape. A frank reminder of his own damned, futile existence. Maybe he should leave his mother's things in her hands. But he was curious about Merle now too.

'Besides, I have work to do,' she added.

That 'work' didn't include entertaining him. But she was watching him and he realised the thoughtfulness on her face had slid to concern—and compassion. He stiffened. Did she think he was distressed about his father's death? He didn't want her pity.

'You're paid to work the weekends as well?' he asked shortly.

That colour rolled back into her cheeks. 'I thought I may as well get on with it, seeing as I'm to remain hidden.'

'Well, take a moment—let's go and see if there's anything worth saving down there.' He didn't think for a second there was, but if he was wrong he wanted rid of all of it immediately. It was only for Leo and for his cousin Grace that he'd agreed to assess everything before selling. For transparency and honesty. They'd missed out on so much, he'd ensure they weren't short-changed in anything else ever again. The other property sales were already completed and all personal effects had been shipped here for a final sort.

'Apparently the entrance is via a hidden trap door in the back of the pool house,' he added, desperately needing to think about anything other than Leo and Grace and his father's awful shame.

'Seriously?'

'Yes.'

Merle knew this was a Bad Idea, but she couldn't resist. Like the home cinema, she'd only briefly glanced at the pool house earlier in the week, opting to explore the leisure activities as a weekend reward for work done. She'd been keen to assess how much work there was ahead of her because Leo Castle's brief had been sketchy. He hadn't known how many boxes were onsite or even the state of the property. But since Ash's unexpected arrival she'd been confined to the study.

Apparently there was no lazing about with a long weekend lie-in for Ash. Which had meant not for her either. It had been impossible to lie in bed listening to him splash about this morning. It had put all sorts of inappropriate images in her mind—and that was already distracted enough by that shockingly hot dream. She was mortified that she was thinking about him in such an inevitable way. Even right now she was trying not to stare at him and not get bothered by the fact he was still wearing only swim shorts. It was perfectly appropriate attire. This was a holiday home and he'd been swimming all morning, but she was too aware of all that *skin*, and her fingertips tingled with the appalling temptation to touch.

As she followed him she desperately fixated on the stunning grounds. There were a couple of alfresco dining areas—an enormous table overlooked the pool, a sweet setting for two was in the corner, while sun loungers and comfortable chairs were placed in sheltered spots where the views over the bay to the sea beyond were sublime.

'The bunker was put in when the pool and tennis court were done. As far as I can tell from the plans, they dug up the entire area and basically buried a prefabricated structure.' Oblivious to her feverish thoughts, Ash moved aside a rug on the pool house floor. 'According to the notes I have…' He trailed off and pushed on one of the inlaid tiles.

To Merle's astonishment, four of the tiles slid back to reveal a dark cavity. 'Oh, wow. There really is a trap door.' She chuckled. 'It's like something out of a spy movie.'

'I know,' he muttered. 'Ridiculous.'

As she stared down, lights flickered on to reveal a steep flight of stairs.

'Shall we?' He glanced at her with a wicked smile.

Her heart pounded. It was crazy to feel this frisson. 'We leave this open, right?' Merle double-checked.

'Of course,' he answered.

The staircase was so steep she could almost slide down it. At the bottom, Ash pulled open a heavy-looking steel door. Yet more lights flickered on as he walked through. Her heart still thudding, Merle followed.

'Oh, wow.' She gazed about the gleaming space in absolute astonishment. 'Wow. This is…'

'Insane?' He circled around on the spot, shaking his head as he took in the set-up.

This was no weird, prison-like cell or futuristic survival bunker. This was pure luxury—like a plush hotel penthouse.

'You'd *never* know it was here.' She wouldn't have believed it possible. Not when above them was that perfect, smooth, manicured tennis lawn beside the pool. There were no tell-tale lumps or hollows giving away the secret beneath the ground.

'Which is the point, right?' He crossed the room.

'It's big.' Merle slowly followed him across the smooth wooden floors that echoed the warm, coastal luxury of the mansion above ground. Cosy leather sofas furnished the room.

'My father wouldn't have anything less than opulent.'

'How does it smell this fresh when we're this far underground?'

'Good maintenance,' he muttered. 'There's a ventilation system. The control panel is in here…'

Merle tuned out as she took in additional details herself. The wall carefully concealed a series of cupboards providing impressive storage space. Digital frames had lit up, creating 'windows' to a virtual garden. The kitchen was compact yet still luxurious. While every space was utilised, it wasn't crammed. It was, she had to admit, absolutely stunning.

'What was the man thinking, having this installed here?' Ash's growl impinged.

'It is pretty unusual.' She released a helpless laugh.

'Did he think he was in danger or the end of the world was nigh?'

'No.' Ash shook his head. 'I think it was the accessory *du jour* and he wanted to feel superior to his friends in his club. He'd hint and whisper but confirm nothing. My father did like keeping secrets.'

Hearing underlying rancour in his tone, Merle stilled. That edge of emotion flickered in his eyes. It made him even more beautiful. Merle stiffened. *Never* had she thought a man beautiful before... The bunker no longer felt spacious. Or safe. It was scarily exciting.

He rubbed his arm absently as he looked about the luxury lounge.

'Are you cold?' she unthinkingly observed aloud. 'Maybe you should wear more clothes.'

He snapped his head back and turned a wicked smile on her. 'Don't you like to swim?' he teased and stepped towards her. 'It's very warm this afternoon.'

It was *extremely* warm this afternoon. Truthfully, she was melting this second, but she wasn't about to tell him that. She'd lost her ability to speak again and she just knew another scalding blush was mottling her skin.

'You're not a pool person? What about the beach?' He cocked his head and chuckled at her. 'Or is it just bubble baths for you?'

'I didn't want to disturb you,' she muttered.

'Too late, Merle.' A heated glint flickered in his eyes. 'But I've been hogging the pool, haven't I?'

'This is your home. I'm just working here.'

'You're also *living* here. You're not supposed to work all day, you're supposed to have breaks. If you like, I'll vacate the pool area at a time that's convenient to you.'

She met his gaze, stilling when she saw seriousness stealing that glint away. Stupidly another wave of heat overwhelmed her—how could she find him even more attractive just because he was being almost human?

She walked down the narrow corridor, more to escape him than to explore. But fascination and curiosity took hold as she ventured further into the pod. There was a bunk room gorgeously decorated in light colours, a sleek bathroom and beyond that a luxurious bedroom for two. The whole place was pristine and perfect and surprisingly cosy. It would be easy to forget you were deep underground. But then Ash followed her into the room and she remembered just how alone and isolated they were.

'It's better finished than most homes,' she commented, purely to pierce the thickening atmosphere. Certainly it was nicer than the house she'd grown up in. 'For a space likely never to be used, it's extravagant, isn't it?'

He merely nodded. Embarrassed, she realised that for him this wasn't extravagant. He probably thought it sparse, given the luxury he was probably used to.

'Anything archive-worthy?' Ash asked.

'I'm not sure.' She glanced again at the concealed drawers and cupboards. If she were bolder, she'd check them out to see if anything was inside. But being down here was confusing her thinking. With Ash in the luxurious bedroom beside her, it felt as if the space was smaller. Intimate. Inescapable.

Her gaze was unerringly drawn back to him. He was watching her. Too close. The temperature soared. Her lungs squeezed and she swivelled to nervously step past him. She needed to get upstairs so she could breathe again. It wasn't that she was claustrophobic, she was just too close to him. All of her usual reticence and caution had evaporated and she was tempted to act…*wantonly.*

It was imperative to put distance between them. Not because he was dangerous in a threatening way, more that he was too wicked and her own mind was turning towards temptation. She'd avoided temptation all of her life—but then, she'd never been confronted by anything or anyone who ignited it within her like this. But the current of awareness that sparked to life whenever Ash Castle so much as stepped into her line of sight wasn't just unsettling, it was also unstoppable.

'I'll just…' She breathed out, unable to regulate her racing heart. 'I'll just head back up.'

She glanced over again and was instantly snared in the crucible of his attention. She lost time—she didn't know how much—as she strived not to crumble beneath the intensity of his killer eye-contact. Her temperature climbed and her pulse skipped and worst of all she was so sure he *knew.* Yet seconds stopped in the heat of that stare.

'I'll be back up in a moment,' he muttered eventually.

Scalding humiliation flooded her as she scurried towards those steep stairs. That mortifying moment made her even more aware of her internal reaction to him. That raw physical response that was so strong, so primal. She had to get away and get herself under control. She climbed carefully, keeping her eyes fixed on each steep stair. But ten steps from the top she stopped, finally realising that there was no glow of sunlight shining down on her. No space where the hatch had been left open.

'A-Ash?' Sound struggled to emerge from her suddenly tight throat. *'Ash?'*

'Yes?' A second later he appeared on the bottom step. 'What?'

But he could already see. He took the stairs two at a time and in a blink was too close behind her. Her heart galloped as she heard his sharply inhaled breath.

'Merle?'

She could feel him only a step from her now but she couldn't bear to face him as she admitted the awful truth. 'I don't think we can get out.'

CHAPTER FOUR

'Merle…' A low hum of laughter emanated from him. 'What did you *do*?'

'I left it open. I know I left it open.' Merle retreated down a few of the stairs to let Ash try the hatch, even though she was fatalistically certain he wasn't going to be able to open it.

'It must've closed automatically,' he drawled.

'Which means it must open automatically again, right?' she rationalised, striving for calm. 'With some other secret mechanism?'

'Sure,' he agreed, too equably.

But there were no levers or buttons or anything near. 'If this place is that high-tech…isn't there some retinal scan that would unlock the door in seconds?'

He glanced at her then, droll amusement oozing from him. 'And if I had my dad's eyeball in my pocket we could use that. Sadly, I don't.'

Why wasn't he bothered by this the same way she was?

Because he's not bothered by you. Her subconscious whispered the biting truth. Or maybe it was because he knew exactly how to get them out and was merely teasing her?

She narrowed her gaze on him. 'So are we stuck in here for the next sixty years until the nuclear winter has passed?'

'Would that be so terrible?' His eyebrows lifted.

Unable to maintain eye contact, Merle turned and went back downstairs, pretending she was calm but in reality far too aware of him a step behind. Dear heaven, she was stuck deep underground in a luxury dooms-day bunker with billionaire Ashton Castle. Some might consider that a dream come true. But for Merle? In her current mode of *uncontrolled inappropriate lust*…it was a nightmare. She paced across the space that was growing smaller again with every second—where was it he'd said the control panel was?

'I refuse to believe we're stuck. Isn't a bunker all about safety?' Her tongue rattled ahead of her brain. 'There must be a second way out—an emergency exit. What if there was a fire?'

'Bigger than the one currently burning you up, you mean?' He watched her walk back and forth with un-disguised amusement.

She gritted her teeth. She wasn't panicking and be-coming hysterical. Okay, yes, she was panicking. Not because she thought they were going to be stuck in here for ever and *die*. It was a more intense issue terrify-ing her. It was the intimacy of being in here with *him*. And that amused look on his face? A sudden suspicion struck. 'You did this deliberately, didn't you?'

He oh-so-slowly, oh-too-innocently widened his gor-geous amber eyes. 'I wasn't the one who shut the door.'

A wave of indignation swamped her. 'I *didn't*.'

He laughed.

She glared back at him. 'It's not funny.'

'The look on your face is. Honestly, what do you think I'm going to do?'

'Nothing,' she snapped.

It wasn't what *he* was going to do. She didn't think for a second he'd actually make a move on her—not without her explicit acquiescence or invitation. No, the problem was the appalling desire that kept bubbling up from where she'd tried to shove it.

'If it's not me, then what is it? Are you claustrophobic?'

'No,' she muttered, trying to haul her wits together. 'It's nothing major. I'm just…'

'You don't trust yourself to be alone with me any more?'

She stilled and glared at him. Of all the arrogant—unfortunately *accurate*—things to suggest.

'You said yourself you've been avoiding me.' His smile broadened. 'And…' He waved a hand at her boiler suit.

She sighed dramatically. 'My clothing choice has nothing to do with you or anyone else. I find it comfortable to work in.'

'No shorts on a hot day?'

'I'm usually in a dusty warehouse.' She was suddenly determined to somehow flip this so he was the one feeling as if *he* was the bug beneath the magnifying glass in the sun and about to frizzle to death. Make *him* feel desperate to escape the bunker. 'Do you ever wear anything *other* than black swim shorts?'

He laughed. 'I do, as it happens. When I'm at work I wear a suit.'

'It's very considerate of you to cover up all your muscles so your poor workers aren't distracted.'

He glanced at the spark in her eye. 'Why, Merle, stop it, you'll make me blush.'

'Is that possible?'

'Probably not.' He grinned.

What was she thinking, talking to him like this? It didn't help that she was starving. She'd not had lunch for fear of running into him and somehow the afternoon had slid away from her. Eager for distraction, she opened the first of the many sleek cupboards in the kitchen area. To her amazement—and relief—there were packets and packets of food. 'Oh, wow, these supplies are amazing.'

'Amazing?' He sounded appalled. 'It's all tins and bottles.'

'It could be worse.' She shot him a sideways look. 'There could be instant noodles.'

'True. That would be terrible.'

'You've obviously never cooked them properly.' She pulled out a tin of peanuts and opened it. The sooner she stabilised her blood sugar, the sooner she got a grip on her crazy hot thinking, right? And if she stuffed her mouth full she'd stop saying things she really shouldn't. And usually wouldn't, but for Ash Castle's influence.

'Are you hungry?' He was still watching her with unconcealed amusement. 'I guess that's not surprising, given you've not been eating anything decent.'

She paused chewing long enough to shoot him another death look.

'Instant noodles are for starving students,' he opined. 'This is not the place for them. I won't allow it.'

'You won't *allow* it?'

'It's unnecessary. Didn't you notice the delivery arrive earlier?' he asked. 'Or are you only interested in the contents of the wine cellar?'

Heat flooded her. 'Mr Castle said—'

'I know what Leo said.' Ash rolled his eyes. 'I also know that if you'd had any idea of the cost you would never have opened it.' He cocked his head. 'Have dinner with me tonight.'

She nearly choked on the next nut. 'Dinner?'

'Yes. Dinner,' he repeated calmly. 'I refuse to work round the clock and definitely not on the weekend. And it's silly for us to avoid each other completely and waste resources cooking two separate meals.'

'You don't seem the type who has to worry about wasting resources.'

'I'm doing my bit for the planet, Merle,' he countered limpidly. 'It's always better to share.'

His echo of last night's words made her skin sizzle. But last night she'd turned and walked out on him without replying. His soft, mocking laughter had trailed her all the way up the stairs to her room. Now she had no choice but to stay and face him. To better him with her own wits. Somehow.

'Say you'll have dinner with me and I'll be inspired to remember the code to open that door,' he said.

So he did know the code. She ground the nuts between her teeth, hard. 'There's a century's worth of food in here,' she said after swallowing. 'I don't need your dinner. I can just stay put.'

His eyes glinted. 'You'd choose to be stuck with me for ever? Isn't that a hellish proposition?'

It was an appallingly appealing proposition. Since when had she become a masochist—to want to remain stuck inside a spacious yet small-feeling safe room that was so *not* safe—at least not for her peace of mind. Or her libido. Or her self-control.

'Besides,' he added, 'there's no *fresh* food. I do like it fresh, sweetheart.'

Merle summoned the little self-control she had left. 'Are you really going to keep me locked in here until I agree to have dinner with you? Doesn't that seem a little coercive? I wouldn't have thought you'd have to resort to abduction tactics.'

'Abduction?' That wicked glint flared in his gaze. 'Asking for a dinner date is nothing,' he said softly. 'It could be far worse. I could demand a kiss for the key code.'

She stilled. 'You wouldn't dare.'

'*I'm* not the one afraid to be daring, sweetheart.'

He was the most aggravating man alive. *This* was what he wanted—for her to rise to his provocation. Well, perhaps she would—just not in the way he wanted. Couldn't she teach him a lesson? Admittedly, she had little likelihood of success. She was a lamb against a lion. But there was something beyond irresistible about the prospect of putting him in his place.

'Merle?' He leaned against the counter as he watched her staring at him. 'What are you thinking?'

His hands were loose, his expression neutral, but his awareness had flared. She felt it too. It locked them both into position—on edge. *Ready.*

'I'm thinking…' she mused softly, 'that who dares, wins.'

'Do you dare?' he drawled. 'Is that what I can see in your eyes?'

He was so bold. And somehow *she* was emboldened. Because she'd pull back at the last moment. She'd tease him and win.

'What you can see,' she said softly, 'is frustration with your insistence on strutting around in nothing but...' She gestured at his swim shorts.

His eyebrows skyrocketed and she felt a ridiculous pleasure that she'd surprised him. She'd surprised herself too. And quite liked it.

'Then look the other way,' Ash taunted. 'I'm not going to change the way I dress for you, sweetheart. Just as I don't expect you to change the way you dress for me.'

A molten sensation stormed through her. She was never dressing *for* him, or anyone. She refused to think about what he thought of her appearance. She already knew he loathed her coverall.

'It's not appropriate,' she argued anyway.

'I'm on holiday at a beach house, Merle,' he said blandly. 'I've been in the pool most of the day.'

Yes, she was *acutely* aware of that fact.

'This whole thing isn't appropriate,' she continued, on a roll now. 'You're my employer.'

'I most definitely am *not*,' he answered instantly. '*Leo* is paying you. I have nothing to do with that.'

She met his fierce gaze and his lips curved in an inviting smile.

'Come closer, Merle. I dare you.'

'Do you really think I'll respond to such little provocation?'

His shoulders lifted and, despite that lazily wicked smile, intensity burned in his eyes. 'Beats me, but I really hope so.'

That absolute honesty stole the wind from her sails.

'You *would* have to be the most outrageous man I've ever met,' she said, breathing out in annoyance.

'Yeah? I bet I'm also the most honest. And here's my truth, Merle. I've been thinking about kissing you every bit as much as you've been thinking about kissing me.'

'I have *not*...' But she blushed at the complete lie.

'No?' He grinned triumphantly. 'It's only chemistry. Nothing more meaningful than a few compounds that spark when struck together. I know you don't actually *like* me.'

'*Like* you?' She rolled her eyes. 'You just want me to disagree and say you're actually not that arrogant, not that inappropriate, not that *appalling*. I'm not falling for it.'

He merely laughed. 'That still doesn't mean you don't want me.'

The cockiness of the man was astounding. 'You're swaggering round, practically naked, like you're some sort of sex gift to the nearest woman—'

'I think you're awfully judgmental about people's clothing.' He flipped to pious with a blink of his unfairly long eyelashes. 'It's personal expression, Merle.'

'Oh, please, you were the one trashing my "forensics fashion".'

'I know, and I was wrong.' He nodded. 'And I've decided, upon reflection, that it's appealing. There's an allure of discovery in what lies beneath.' His lips quirked. 'Of course, I already know the visual delights to be seen under yours…'

She burned with embarrassment. She should have turned down his invitation to explore the bunker. Avoidance wasn't just the best solution for dealing with this man, it was the *only* solution. Except, much to her annoyance, Ash Castle was easy to like. He was sharp and funny and she knew he took pleasure in deliberately provoking her. He didn't mean most of this talk—there was that spark in his eye, a devilish gleam knowing he was taking it too far. Frankly, she was enjoying trying to better him. It was a game she'd never played. A game she wanted to win.

And now? Now there was a part of her that wanted nothing more than to wipe that smug challenge off his face and topple his assurance the way he'd obliterated hers.

The way he watched her was unashamedly interested, underlined with curiosity. She was different, that was all. Not like the other women who slid into his bed with ease. Surely she couldn't be the only woman ever to have said no to him?

He outstretched his arms and took hold of the counter's edge. 'I promise I won't let go, so you can be assured there'll be no wandering hands. Then you can get it out of your system.'

She was sure he was joking. Yet he was still and serious and she had to dig her heels in to stop the temptation slithering through her. Somehow time blipped, somehow she stepped nearer. A hard blaze lit his eyes and she couldn't tear her gaze from him.

'A kiss for the key code? Is that the deal?' she asked.

'If that's the deal you want to make.'

'And dinner?'

'Is happening regardless and it will be a much more leisurely, sumptuous affair than instant noodles followed by a bite of pudding.' His eyes gleamed as he waited, alert, for her response.

His confidence was extreme. He was certain in his arrogant assumption that she wouldn't dream of turning him down. Truth was, she didn't want to refuse him. In any of these things. But she would.

'Just a little closer, Merle,' he whispered with full arrogance on display. 'What's the worst that could happen?'

There were so many worsts that she could think of. He could laugh. Humiliate her. Tell her he hadn't meant it. Hadn't she had that experience before—to be led along a path by a handsome man, only to have him humiliate her publicly? Proving her grandmother's ridiculously dire warnings that men were to be avoided.

Only, there was an intensity in Ash's expression that she couldn't turn away from, and he was so very still that she couldn't resist stepping that breath closer.

She would whisper 'never' to him. She would refuse to give him any kind of satisfaction. 'I ought to…'

'To what?' He breathed heavily.

She couldn't remember what she'd been going to do any more. Her brain had shut down.

'Run,' he finished for her in a raw, low growl of bitter honesty. 'That's what you should do, Merle. You should turn around and run, right now.'

Maybe she should. But a flare of need had unfurled. Because she knew he'd meant it, but she also knew it was the last thing he wanted. It was the last thing she wanted too.

He wasn't smiling any more. All that laughing arrogance, all the careless flirting, had vanished and all that remained was that almost angry look in his eyes as he fiercely stared, as if trying to compel her with his thoughts. Even with his arms stretched wide, his biceps were flexed as he gripped the bench tightly. But that stance made him vulnerable. She could get close to his body.

'Why did you dare me, then?' Her own anger bloomed. 'To *make* me run? To prove my cowardice? To put this all on me so you don't have to answer for it?'

Was he trying to prove that her inexperience was something to be embarrassed about? And that it was her own fault? That there was something wrong with her?

'Merle.' His mutter was almost an apology.

It changed everything again. The intensity between them shifted to something more than sensual. Something devastatingly intimate. And emotional. Anger—and another emotion too powerful to ignore— overwhelmed her into action. She rose on tiptoe and held his gaze. Feeling fire scurrying along her veins, she was about to tell him exactly what she thought of him. Except she was frozen. Less than an inch away from him, she suddenly couldn't move.

Yet his heat emanated, burning her, inexorably pulling her closer. And then he tucked in his chin, lowering his head just enough for their lips to brush. It was little more than a swift press but a shock of pleasure struck her insides. She felt taut as a bowstring, ready to fire. But she didn't. She pulled away, immediately hoping he'd take it as a mockery of the real thing—that she'd offered only a pretence, given his request was so outrageous.

'No,' he muttered hoarsely. 'Come back.'

Not a line. Not an arrogant command. A raw plea that escaped gritted teeth.

She hadn't exactly gone anywhere. Only a breath away, she could see the warmth of his eyes, more mesmerising than ever. Whoever wanted to step into a crucible? To willingly fling themselves into flames? But these were searing licks of pleasure. These were irresistible.

'My turn.' He bent his head closer.

Still, she didn't step away. Even when she'd told herself that was exactly what she was going to do—veer close, only to swerve at the last minute. Like some game of chicken. Only she'd discovered that a collision was the far more preferable option.

'Just stay there,' he growled. 'Just for a minute.'

They were close enough for their mouths to brush as he spoke. For her to feel his warmth, his breath on her skin. She could feel him watching her, feel the light nuzzle of his nose against hers. Gentle, careful. Searingly sensual. It only took the tiniest lift of her chin to catch his lips again and hers clung to his without conscious intent. But then—without releasing that counter— he somehow moved, somehow took control.

His mouth roved over hers, gentle, then with a subtly increasing strength. She closed her eyes, lost in the kiss instantly. She leaned closer and inadvertently grazed her fists against his bare skin. The sizzle was intoxicating and she unfurled her fingers, shivering at his scorching heat. And then she simply melted. Her belly pressed against his, her palms spread on his solid chest and her head fell back as she let him kiss her to life. It was pure electric vitality now crackling through her veins. She heard the low groan from the back of his throat and an answering echo, a moan from deep within, escaped her.

Both sounds impinged on her mind, dragging her back to reality. Stunned at the intensity and speed with which she'd lost herself, she tore away, snapping the contact.

This time he didn't try to stop her. He just watched, his beautiful eyes lit by his potent, wild spirit. A cloud of sensuality wafted from him, tempting her to get close again. Not a cloud—*chains*. If she wasn't careful she might be locked in his thrall for good.

There wasn't satisfaction on his face. Nor the smug arrogance she'd expected because he'd got what he wanted. Got it so easily. If anything, he seemed as breathless, as speechless as she. But that was impossible.

Breathing hard, she broke free of those invisible bonds and stepped back. She didn't want him to know how deeply that had affected her. She'd spent so many years hiding by staying silent. For once, she was going to have to speak up to cover up. She was going to have to pretend.

'I've changed my mind.' She expelled a shaky breath. 'I don't need your key code. I've come to consider the bunker a safe haven. I'll happily stay down here.'

A smile spread across his face and that arrogance gleamed. 'You were that moved, huh?' He nodded. 'So now you're too scared to have dinner with me.' He lifted his hands from the bench and shook them. 'Has that one kiss made you too frightened of what else you might find yourself wanting to do?'

That was so accurate she wanted to hit him.

He stepped forward. 'Do you really think you'd be safer now, stuck in here with me? In this teeny, tiny space?'

'It's not that tiny,' she said, desperately defending her position, and decided to appeal to his humanity. 'And I really think you're not the animal you make yourself out to be. You're not that desperate for anything.'

'No?' He half laughed. 'I'm glad you're so certain. Because I'm not. And now I can't escape the sight or scent of you? Now I've had a taste?'

He stalked towards her, but at the final moment, when she was bracing for impact, he swerved and stepped past her—pulling off the move she'd planned but failed to perform.

And the sudden sense of loss? Of disappointment? In that second she hated her own body—the chemicals and hormones that had been so thoroughly turned *on*. She watched him viciously prod a discreet panel in the study area of the living space. Only a second later she heard a hissing sound and the clang of some mechanism.

'The door's open, Merle.' Ash glanced at her. 'I suggest you return to the real world.'

CHAPTER FIVE

THE PROBLEM WAS that the 'real world' was no different. Above ground, breathing fresh air, forcing physical distance, Ash still wanted her more than he'd wanted any woman ever. He rolled his shoulders, unable to release the tension that had been building since the second he'd first seen her. Tension that was now unbearable after he'd touched her. What had begun as the most chaste kiss of his life had ended as the most unforgettable. How was it possible that he'd been left aching with such desperation? It wasn't like anything he'd experienced before. It was no lie that he'd needed to get them out of there as fast as possible.

When she'd professed her desire to stay locked down there? He'd had to move before he took her up on it.

Ordinarily, most kisses didn't end like that. Not so suddenly. Not with his lover walking away. Ordinarily, most kisses ended with all clothes off and multiple orgasms on. Not with Merle Jordan though. Of course it couldn't be ordinary with her.

She was so tantalising. He'd never been as careful, absurdly terrified that he'd scare her off somehow. But then he'd lost track of any planned seduction. His mind had hazed. All that had remained was sensation in that sweet, scorching moment when he'd had his mouth on hers. Then she'd put her hands on him.

There'd always been a clinical element to Ash's conquests. A decision to accept the offer of some mindless, emotionless physical relief and pleasure. This was different. This was a visceral ache in his core. Desire he couldn't deny. Every other time it had been easy enough to walk away. Now he couldn't. It wasn't because he was trapped here. For all his hedonism, all his copious enjoyment of easy pleasure, he'd never been so fixated. Now he feared he was on the edge. That he'd do almost anything to have Merle Jordan in his bed was a frankly alarming feeling.

And there'd been inexperience in her kiss. Ash didn't fool around with women who didn't know the score. Not since he'd broken a young woman's heart a decade ago. He didn't like to think of Rose but her visage flickered in his mind. Of course it did—his treatment of Rose had been the reason for his mother's anger here, that afternoon when his whole world had been turned upside down.

He slammed the door on those recollections. Things were very different now. While Merle's initial shyness had reminded him of Rose, she'd shown herself to be very different just beneath the surface. Merle wasn't some sweet-sixteen, never-been-kissed, awkward girl. She was an adult—fully capable of handling this attraction and of standing up to him more devastatingly than most people he'd met. He knew she wanted nothing more than to put him properly in his place. And when she let her tongue off the leash? When she was provoked enough not to hold back?

He wanted that too. Because he wanted her. But, given the inexperience that he intuitively sensed, he needed her to come to him. He *needed* her to be more than sure. He needed her to be in charge. Instead, she'd vanished back into that study.

He paced through to the kitchen, grumpily fixing on the perfect displacement activity. He was no great cook but he also wasn't afraid to source expert help when necessary. Seeing those little puddings of hers last night had made his mouth water, so he'd been deliberate in the groceries he'd ordered for delivery from one of the local delis this morning. He'd tempt every one of her tastebuds until she could do nothing but ask for more.

Ninety minutes later, he appeared at the door to the study where she was still hiding.

'Hey, darling.' He leaned against the doorjamb. 'Dinner's ready.'

Merle had spent the afternoon locked back in the study, buried in the boring business papers from his father's box, keeping calm and carrying on as if nothing drastically life-changing had happened. But Ash hadn't gone back to his usual routine. He hadn't appeared at the pool to swim for endless hours. She wished he had. The truth was, she'd realised, she wanted to swim *with* him.

But now he led her to a beautifully set small table overlooking the pool. It offered spaciousness, room to escape, a stunning view across the bay and an even better view across the table—to him.

Merle gazed down at the vibrantly coloured curry instead. 'This looks amazing. Thank you.'

She perched, keenly aware of the awkward silence that immediately descended, but she was unable to think of anything to break it. *Don't be pathetic.* She chewed, furious at overthinking everything. Why couldn't she relax? Why couldn't she shut down that searing, shockingly sexual response?

Merle didn't have sexual responses to anyone. Why now, with such a known playboy who took nothing and no one seriously? Perhaps that was the problem. Had his reputation sparked a primal response within her subconscious? Had she inherited some genetic predisposition to bounders? She'd always rejected the way her grandmother had labelled her mother—as a foolish woman who'd 'fallen' and brought shame on the family by getting pregnant, unmarried and young—yet that lingering burn curled through her as she heard the strident echo of her grandmother's displeasure.

Stay away from men. You don't want to make the same mistake as your mother.

Everyone made mistakes. Having sex wasn't necessarily one of them. Merle knew her mother was brave and loyal and loving. And frankly, it would be nice to have a sexual response to someone *some time*. Temptation whispered, telling her that an experience with Ash Castle might be perfect, might teach her much, *without* costing her heart. She desperately needed to stop thinking about any of this. She'd initiate a safe conversation instead. The one topic she had in common with him was her work.

'Is there anything in particular you would like me to

do with the diaries?' she asked, pleased to have thought of something innocuous to discuss.

'Diaries?' He glanced up.

'Your father's diaries. I found a few in one of the boxes today.'

His mouth compressed and emotion flared in his eyes. 'Direct any questions on his things to Leo. He's the one paying you.'

'But—'

'I don't want to know about it,' he clipped. 'As far as I'm concerned you can burn it all.'

Merle focused on her plate, taking a moment to digest his snap.

He sighed heavily. 'Don't look at me like that.'

'I'm not looking at you,' she answered equably.

'Exactly.' He half-laughed, half-groaned and then sighed. 'Do you really enjoy cataloguing the detritus of people's meaningless lives?'

Oh, wow, there was some bitterness to unravel there.

'Yes, I do,' she said calmly. 'Archives of all sorts, records of people's thoughts and experiences, are valuable.'

'In what possible way?' he asked as if any valid reason was impossible.

'It's the connection to the past, isn't it? Things tether us, help us learn things about our heritage.' She hesitated. 'Sometimes I deal with the records or things other people can't bear to face yet,' she said softly. 'I put them in an order so they're there when people are ready.'

'And if they're not?'

'I put a date on each box for when the contents will

be reassessed. If it's deemed no longer valuable it goes to a secure facility to be destroyed.'

His lips twisted. 'That sounds perfect. Make the date tomorrow.'

She shook her head. 'Not in the protocol, sorry.'

'There's a protocol?'

'Sure,' she said softly, but firmly. 'Because these things matter.'

'They really don't.'

She held his gaze.

He cocked his head and blinked. 'You think I'm protesting too much.'

She hesitated. 'I think strong feelings provoke strong reactions.'

'Oh, indeed.' He stared at her for another pregnant moment. 'You're assuming that what's written in those diaries is even true.'

'Actually, I'm not assuming anything. Of course, a historian would study other sources to confirm if one person's account of things is true. But I don't have to worry about that, and discovering dead people's secrets is something I enjoy.' She mirrored his cock of the head and blinked back at him. 'Those of the living too, actually.'

'Allow me to disappoint you early, darling. I don't have any secrets. Secrets are never any fun, despite what others will try to tell you. Take that bunker—it's an unnecessary, expensive monstrosity. And it wasn't my father's only secret. Nor was it the biggest in his life, unfortunately.' Ash coolly reeled off a list. 'Illegitimate offspring. Hidden bank accounts. Shady dealings.' His blandness was too studied. 'And for years I had no idea. It's amazing how little you can know someone even when you live under the same roof.' His direct gaze seared through her. 'Maybe you'll know him better than I did once you're done. Or maybe, as I said, you should just burn it all.'

She was curious about *him* right now, not his father. 'Everyone has *some* secrets.'

'My family life was a family lie,' he said. 'Which I hated. So if I'm going to do something, I'm going to do it with full transparency. No secrecy. No shame. No regrets,' he said with proud finality. 'That's why it's a good thing my half-brother is now in charge of my father's company, not me. Leo's the responsible one. He'll keep an eye out for those employees. Ironic, isn't it? That the child my father denied for so long is the one willing and able to preserve all he built.' He glanced down at his steaming curry and then looked back up at her, his expression even more alert than usual. 'Do you have family treasures of your own?' he asked. 'A mountain of old letters and recipe books and chipped china?'

Merle didn't answer. She'd had to sell everything to afford the care bills for her grandfather, and now she was homeless she had no space to store anything big anyway. But she'd always found solace in *other* old things that she had no direct connection to. Not that she was about to tell deeply cynical Ash Castle that; he'd only scoff.

'Things can be destroyed, Merle,' Ash drawled, proving her point immediately. 'What's the point in holding on to things so tightly when, with a strike of a match, they can be lost for ever?'

'Says a man who accumulates more things than most people.'

'Only money,' he corrected.

'People can be lost too,' she muttered.

'So *things* are sometimes safer than people?' he asked astutely. 'Is that why you surround yourself with them?'

'What makes you think I do?' Her defensiveness rose.

'You spend your days prioritising and protecting material things from other people's pasts,' he asserted. 'But not around actual, real live people.'

She tilted her chin at him, feeling that frisson—that kick from his light teasing. 'And here *you* are,' she said pointedly, 'avoiding actual, real live people.'

'It's a momentary hiatus, not a *habit*, for me.'

'Well.' She breathed softly, absorbing the hit. 'We *all* have bad habits, Ash.'

She took a mouthful of the curry, feeling her taste-buds zing. But her nerves were zinging all the more from the appreciative grin he flicked her. Suddenly, he pushed back from the table.

'I've forgotten something vital.'

Before she could question what, he went inside. She took the chance to release a breath she'd not realised she'd been holding. Instinctively, she knew they were dancing around something more serious than either of them wanted to recognise. Maybe she ought not to open the lid on those hurts, yet she couldn't resist her curiosity.

He returned brandishing a bottle of champagne. She eyed it warily. 'Is it as expensive as that other one?'

'More.' He laughed negligently and popped the cork. 'Will you help me drink it?'

'I imagine you could manage it on your own.'

'Are you referring to my insatiable appetite?'

That awareness fizzed inside her, the bubbling sensation mirroring the miniature ones in the glass. She lifted the glass he filled for her and took a haughty sip because he'd set a challenge she didn't have the strength—or will—to ignore.

Ash had tried to distract himself by mucking about in the kitchen, but now she was sitting across the table and it felt like the most intimate date he'd had in years. Which was crazy, because it wasn't really a date. They were just two people staying in the same house sharing dinner. His body begged to differ. His brain? That needed respite from the edginess in their conversation. They'd veered close to topics he didn't discuss. He needed to raise shields, and to do so he fell back on customary form—to be outrageous and turn this to a totally superficial skin-to-skin tease. He'd make the most of their chemistry. It was the perfect distraction.

'Are we going to talk about it?' he asked bluntly. The colour in her cheeks deepened in that gorgeous way. 'The kiss, I mean.'

She sipped her champagne to avoid answering.

'Don't worry, darling,' he purred. 'You're not the first woman I've rendered speechless.'

'Well, *you* are the most arrogant man I've met,' she said calmly—no flirtation couched in mock-outrage.

'Am I?' He grinned and went in search of some truth. 'Or maybe it's just that you've not met many men.'

'Actually I've met several arrogant jerks over the years.' She lifted her chin. 'You're by far the worst.'

Again, no hyperbole. Just a calm, direct comment. Ash stifled his surprise. Somehow he'd imagined her to be a complete innocent—permanently hidden away from the eyes and attentions of other men, like some Rapunzel trapped in a tower of archival boxes. But she'd met several guys? When? Who?

'The thing is, you don't have to be,' she said, derailing his curiosity. 'You attract women easily.' She angled her head and a gleam shone in her deep eyes. 'Of course, mostly it's your bank account,' she said flatteningly. 'But your looks help. And your confidence to a degree. You just take it too far.'

His looks? His confidence *to a degree*? He was used to women being attracted to him and to all kinds of attempts at flirtation or to capture his interest. But sweet, shy Merle's serene stocktake of his eligible bachelor qualities didn't feel like a flirtation attempt. The realisation was both refreshing and disappointing.

'But the "one night" thing that you admitted to last night,' she added. 'That's purely for *self*-preservation.'

'You're incorrect,' he drawled. 'That's for *their* benefit. I'm not a marrying man, Merle. I never will be.'

'Oh, really?' She pouted and looked downcast. 'Perhaps I'll learn to live with the disappointment, eventually.'

He chuckled. 'Miaow.'

Her lashes lifted and those deep brown eyes stared soulfully into his. 'As if that's not the reaction you wanted.'

What he *wanted* was becoming untenable. Not to mention impossible.

It was his turn to take another sip of champagne to buy time. Easy banter usually stood him in good stead. He enjoyed setting the mark and establishing the very basic rules he lived by. He generally glided towards the inevitable conclusion that chemistry such as this inspired. It was all anticipation—in the parry and thrust of prospective pleasure. But Merle seemed determined to stamp out the sparks showering between them with absurdly prim, pragmatic denial. Didn't she know desire like this could only be destroyed by as explosive means as possible? The frankly animal urge to reach out and rouse her spirit disturbed him. For the first time he was truly trapped by lust. And it was *crazy*.

'You're blushing.' He was so tense he sounded husky.

'It's the champagne,' she muttered.

'It's not the champagne,' he muttered back.

She lifted her chin with a defiance that undermined itself with its own fierceness. 'It's not you either.'

'Then there's only one thing remaining.'

'And that is…?'

'You.' He smiled as triumph roared at the realisation. '*You're* bothering yourself.'

Her flush receded, leaving her a little pale, but her gaze didn't shy from his. 'Is that something you're familiar with?'

Clever woman, wasn't she? Reflecting his barb back at him and forcing a fragment of honesty to escape from beneath his veneer. 'Sure. I get very sick of myself.' He stiffened. 'But I know how to escape my own thoughts.'

'Via rakish escapades?' Her gaze was relentless.

'Rakish?' He chuckled at her old-fashioned terminology. 'Why not? There are worse ways, I think.' He cocked his head and challenged her. 'What are you going to do to escape your thoughts, Ms Prim?'

'Just because I won't slither beneath your spell, you say I'm prim. *Really?*'

She was opting for diversion—setting up another superficial spar to escape answering with actualities. He knew the gambit well, as he'd played it many times himself.

'Don't worry, I'm not taking it personally.' He smiled. 'Because I don't think it's just me—I don't think you'd slither beneath *anyone* in any great hurry.'

She tossed her head to the side. 'Because no one would want me to?'

Actually no, that wasn't at all what he'd meant. The flash of vulnerability on her face let him know that wasn't a play for compliments. In fact, he'd scored an unintended foul. The vein of rejection that everyone had apparently ran particularly deep within her. *Why?* Protectiveness—that rare sensation for him—surged.

'We both know one guy who definitely wants you to,' he muttered almost angrily. 'And there's no way I'd *ever* be the only one.'

'This is what you do, is it?' she asked. 'Flatter any female in the vicinity. Is it a compulsion to seduce everyone into liking or wanting you?'

Was that the effect he was having on her? He hoped so. But he realised she didn't believe he actually meant what he'd said about her. 'So judgmental, Merle. Why?'

He waited as she looked down at the empty plate before her, hiding her mesmerising eyes from him. Then she glanced back up and he saw a new bitterness in the heat of her rich gaze.

'I'm jealous of you.'

Surprise silenced him.

'You swing through life, apparently not giving a damn about anything, yet getting *everything* you want.'

'I've already told you I work for what I get,' he pointed out.

'In business, sure. But in your love life?'

'Love life?' He scoffed. 'I don't have a *love* life.'

'Sex life, then. It comes so easily to you. You have no idea how hard it is for normal people.' She paused. 'Shy people.'

That hot wave of protectiveness washed over him again, only this time it was merged with an equally powerful surge of possessiveness. *Both* feelings were foreign. Both were undeniable. 'All you have to do is ask, Merle. All you have to do is say yes. Have you ever done either?'

Colour swept over her skin and clued him in to her true status.

'Never *ever*?' His eyes widened. 'Not to anyone for anything?'

'I went on a date once.'

'Once?' Prim wasn't the word for her. But something compressed his chest, a premonition of her pain. 'You were hurt?'

Her attention flashed back to him. 'Only my pride.'

He was relieved, but that underlying irritative effect she had on him flared up again. 'So because that happened *once*, you've not said yes again?'

She shrugged dismissively. 'No one's ever asked again.'

She'd been ignored? No. His gaze narrowed and he slowly shook his head. 'Maybe that's because you work locked away in isolated rooms with only old, dusty things for company. How do you expect to meet anyone if you don't go where the living are? I bet you've never downloaded any dating apps.'

She bet *he* never had either. Merle shuddered at the thought of trying to make herself sound attractive on an app in twenty words. 'What would you have me do? Wear a tiny bikini and pout in a profile pic?'

Annoyed by him and by her own wayward thoughts, she stood and carried the plates inside to the kitchen with ruthless efficiency, as if she could wipe this heated awkwardness away like harmless crumbs.

'Merle—'

'I've something to show you,' she interrupted. Distraction all the way.

She'd prove to him things from the past were worth preserving. That slightly wicked gleam lit in his eyes again and she had to catch her laugh. She went back down the corridor to the study. It only took a minute to grab the boxes she'd found and bring them back to the kitchen. 'Look at these—it's an amazing collection. I think they're all vintage.'

She put them on the bench in front of him. There were a number of traditional games—chess, snakes and ladders, dice games and puzzles. Glancing up, she saw he'd paled slightly.

'Where'd you find those?' he asked gruffly.

'In a cupboard in the study.'

'Curious thing, aren't you?' His gaze was locked on the games in front of him. Tension bracketed his sensual mouth, stealing away his customary smile.

'It's my job to notice interesting things tucked away in dark corners,' she answered lightly. 'Someone did a good job of collecting these. They would have been hard to find. Especially in such good condition as this— they'll be worth a lot. This compendium alone is worth thousands.' She placed the last antique wooden box down carefully.

'They weren't collected for their value,' Ash said softly. 'They were my mother's.'

'Your mother's?'

He now reached for the nearest. 'I thought they were long lost.' He frowned. 'Everything else of hers seems to…'

Merle paused, unsure how to respond.

'All those things in the boxes you're sorting,' he added softly. 'All the art, the books, the collections. They're all his, right?'

Her heart sank at the hurt in his voice. She'd not meant to upset him, merely distract him. 'I'm sorry—'

'Don't be. I'm glad the games are still here.' A half-smile tugged his lips. 'She loved a challenge.'

Merle was intrigued. 'Was she a risk-taker, too?'

'Oh, she was a player and she liked to win.'

'So that's where you get it from.' Merle glanced up when she heard his choking laugh. She was stupidly pleased to see his smile return.

'She made a couple of bad bets in her life,' he said. 'Her husband being one of them. She had a chronic health condition, so she wasn't on the sports sidelines when I was a kid. She had a lap table she'd set up on her bed and we'd play. Board games, puzzles, cards.' He lifted the lid off one box and ran a finger across the wooden counters. 'I haven't seen these in for ever.'

It took a moment for everything he'd just said to really sink in. How sad for his mother and for him. Yet they'd had good times.

'So which was your favourite?' she asked. 'Which are you best at?'

She saw that dangerous, playful light in the amber.

'You want to play with me, Merle?'

'A *board* game,' she stressed. 'Why not?'

'It's not too much of a risk for you?'

'I think you have your own code of conduct.'

'High praise,' he mocked. 'You think I play around, but I play by the rules.'

'*Your* rules, yes. One night, right?'

He drew back and shot her a serious look. 'No cheating. No children. No commitment. Fun and done.'

'In that one night? Truly? You don't ever want more with someone?'

'What is more, Merle?' he asked sardonically. 'It's only messy.'

'What's so wrong with mess?'

'People are greedy. And selfish. Everyone is, at heart. Especially me.'

'I think that's just an excuse,' she said cheerfully. 'To make it easier for you. You don't even have to *try* to be better.'

He laughed then drew in a steadying breath. 'You want to see if you can beat me, Merle?'

'I'm not afraid to *try*.' She lifted her chin. 'A *board* game.'

Satisfaction flared between them both.

'You pick the game,' he ordered. 'I want you to have some kind of chance.'

'Snakes and ladders,' she said promptly. It was the only one she actually knew the rules to. 'A roll of the dice and you can win or lose.'

'You're relying purely on chance? You're not willing to back yourself and pick a strategy game?'

'Who says you can't have strategy in snakes and ladders?' She scooped up the dice and shook them in her hand.

'You're not going to kiss them?' he teased.

'I don't think that will bring me any extra luck.' She rolled and made the first move on the board.

'Kiss mine for me,' he jeered.

She puckered and made a loud popping sound with a fake kiss. He promptly rolled double sixes.

'Thanks, darling.'

She didn't reply. She was too busy fuming at the man's luck. That wicked grin spread over his face as he counted out the spaces he got to move—landing on a ladder, naturally enough. Three rolls along she rolled the dice and found herself on the head of a snake and slid back to the beginning again, while he was already onto his next move.

'You play a fast game,' she noted. 'Barely taking the time to consider your options.'

'Because I know what I need to do.' He slid his counter on the board and lifted his intense gaze to hers. 'Look at that,' he said softly. 'I won.'

'Wasn't it inevitable, given you're so much more experienced?' She gazed across the game to meet his intense stare.

'If you're not used to playing games, why are you so willing to try?' he asked.

'Because there's always hope, right? There's always a chance there might be an *exception*.'

'You want to risk everything on chance? On the possibility of being an exception?' He shook his head and laughed. 'Maybe you're more of a risk-taker than most.'

He was wrong. Yet once again she was tempted to take all the risks with him. Once again she was a hot mess of confusion and conflict. Of desire and denial. And of silence.

He cocked his head and smiled slowly as he studied her with that relentless intensity. 'I bet I know what the troubling thoughts are.'

'Do not, I beg, reveal your appalling arrogance yet again.'

For him it was merely an entertaining escape, but for her it was pure, tantalising mystery.

He leaned back. 'You can't stop thinking about that kiss any more than I can.'

Was he really thinking about it? Or was that one of his many practised lines? *Did it really matter?* Because for her it was the truth. He was magnetic.

'Why not a repeat?' he asked.

'There are so many reasons,' she muttered. 'But I think you just want what you can't have,' she said. 'You want the woman who doesn't want you.'

'Is that what you think you are?' He chuckled. 'I've met many women who didn't want me and I've never felt the need to persuade them otherwise. You're only saying no because you can't stand to say yes to me. You don't like it when I win, because you think that means you lose,' he muttered. 'But I promise you won't lose. And, if you like, you don't have to say anything at all. You can choose to stand there, or you can move to that other room and have your own space. Your choice. But I know what I want.'

'And you always get it?' She shook her head. 'I don't believe anyone gets what they want all of the time.'

'Then why not get what you want when you *can*,' he suggested with a smile, 'when it's right here, waiting for you to simply admit it?'

He made it sound logical and easy and as if it meant nothing. Which, of course, it did for him.

'You're so annoying,' she muttered feebly.

He stepped closer. 'Why shouldn't you get what *you* want, Merle? Why shouldn't you get to have some fun?'

'A one-time limited offer?' She paused.

'Games end, Merle.'

True. And no matter how he tried to spin it, there was always a winner and a loser. She knew she was nothing but another challenge to him. Once conquered, the challenge of her would be destroyed and his interest would wane. He was mercurial, a creature easily bored. Never truly satisfied.

But *she* could be satisfied. She could finally experience the one thing everyone else in the world seemed to go crazy for. And if the hint she'd had earlier was any indication? It would be so worth it. Couldn't *she* be the winner? But a streak of insecurity undermined the warmth flowing through her. 'Is this because I'm the only woman around for miles? Because we're stuck here together and you need a release? Because you're bored? Because—'

'You're magnificent and fascinating. Because you've snared my interest and I want to work out why. Because I desperately want to make you feel good enough to stop questioning everything and just enjoy our explosiveness.'

His fierce interruption silenced her. Was this explosive for him too, then? Was this something a little less ordinary for him? The prospect tempted that weak part of her.

'There's nothing wrong with sex,' he breathed. 'Did someone tell you there was?'

Merle froze. He'd veered so close to the truth there. She'd tried to mute her grandmother's endless lectures about being 'good', about not bringing shame home. She'd linked shame so explicitly, so wrongly with sex. Her mother's fears for her still echoed too. She'd never seen an example of women allowed to simply have fun, let alone anything loving.

'So there has to be something wrong with me because I'm saying no to you?' She turned defensive.

'But you haven't said no to me yet.' He held up his hands. 'Be *honest*.'

That was an altogether different dare from him.

'I've told you the rules I play by,' he said. 'You know I don't cheat. I don't lie.'

'And I do?'

'To yourself, maybe. Isn't that what you're doing right now?'

Emotions were heightened. Desire was heightened. But so was doubt. She'd been burned before.

'I'll admit we have some chemistry. That doesn't mean I'm going to say yes. I like pudding a lot, but I'm not going to over-indulge because it wouldn't be good for me. There's such a thing as balance.'

'But you're not indulging at all. There's no balance there either.' A smile curved his lips. 'Why don't you just sample a little? You can say "enough" any time you like.' He gestured towards the oven. 'You know there's pudding on offer here tonight.'

She glanced at the oven and laughed. 'I couldn't possibly. I've had sufficient.'

'Oh, Merle,' he chastised softly. 'Since when was *sufficient* ever enough?'

CHAPTER SIX

ARE WE GOING to talk about it?

Not only had Merle never had such kisses to discuss before, but she'd never had anyone to discuss them with either. She'd stayed in the shadows, silent almost all of her life. She'd been taught—by her mother, her grandmother, and her own small experience—that invisible equalled safe and that men meant trouble. But Ash hadn't let her hide. And, while they'd danced with banter and tease, at the core was a challenge for honesty. For her to embrace her own desires. Now seductive possibilities fired her blood, pushing her pulse faster. He was leaving at the end of the week, their paths would never intersect again, no one would ever even know they'd met, no one would ever care—certainly not him. He was a hedonist who lived in the moment and who took advantage of all good opportunities when they arose—in business and in pleasure, right?

Maybe she could learn more than a few things from him.

She paced the length of her suite, unable to unwind. She'd run away after dinner—wary that her feelings were going to topple her into making a rash decision that couldn't be reversed. But wouldn't she be crazy not to claim such a chance? To experience something most other people enjoyed? It wasn't as if she was at risk from him when she knew exactly what she'd be getting. And not getting. She'd not been saving her virginity. It was more that she'd not met any possible takers until now.

Hot and bothered, she ran a cold bath, hoping to relax and settle her runaway thoughts. But she couldn't stop thinking about him. Ash offered brevity, but intensity. A night at his island hideaway. Wouldn't it be a chance for her to freely explore and accumulate one great memory? She didn't need to take everything so seriously, did she?

Because she couldn't ignore this ache. This burning temptation that not even icy water could soothe.

When she finally got out of the bath she heard a splash coming from outside. She glanced out of the window and stilled. Ash was back in the pool, taking a swim at nearly midnight. Occasionally, the light that spilled from the house caught him—making the droplets of water on his body glint like diamonds. Beautiful, powerful, impossible to tame and so tempting. But even as her heart thundered and her blood raced, she stepped back and turned away, too schooled in self-denial.

In silence.

But the tension in her body didn't lessen through the sleepless night. That temptation no longer whispered, it clamoured. She worked in the study all morning, thoughts circling incessantly until a low anger throbbed in time with the building pain in her temples. She was annoyed not by the ideas he'd planted in her head, but by her own cowardice. Her own docility. She was sick of doing as she'd been told half her life. She was sick of staying quiet. She was sick of missing out on what she really wanted. And she was so tired of him swimming in that damned pool, flaunting his perfect body.

She stalked out of the study onto the patio. His magnetism was too strong for her to resist any longer. She wanted to have what she wanted—*who* she wanted. He looked up. The immediate expression in his eyes scorched away the last of her shyness so that certainty flooded her.

He hoisted himself out of the pool in one powerful action, picked up a towel from a lounger and wrapped it round his waist. 'Going to roll the dice, Merle?'

He knew already. But now *he* waited. Yet, by just being near such a source of outrageous vitality, she finally felt emboldened and empowered enough to step from the shadows and speak up.

'I've decided I want…' She broke off, battling the furious blush she felt swamping her skin.

He stood more still than she did. 'Want?'

She breathed out. This still wasn't easy. 'What you dared. You. Here. Now.'

Ash's customary wicked smile didn't light up his face. Instead, he continued to look alarmingly serious. 'You said you never over-indulge and ran away the second I offered dessert.'

She had. She'd turned tail and fled, overwhelmed by the thoughts in her own damned mind. 'You said I don't indulge at all. You were right.'

His gaze locked on her more intently.

'I want to finish what we started in the bunker.' Merle's wish slipped out. 'In fact, I want more.'

He didn't move. He didn't answer. He just stared at her, expressionless.

Merle counted down the achingly slow seconds until doubt exploded in a ball of fire in her stomach. She'd just thrown herself at him and he wasn't reacting at all how she'd anticipated.

'Merle…'

The strained whisper was so unlike him. His tone holding nothing short of…regret?

Merle flinched, mortified. Hadn't she seen the flicker of interest in his eyes just then? Hadn't he spent all of dinner last night tempting and teasing her into saying yes? Cold horror struck as her doubts mushroomed. Had it all been a ploy to see if he could get her to *yes*? Had *that* been his real game? Had it been a prank—with him taking cruel pleasure in seducing her, only to say no?

Had history just repeated itself—only way, way worse? *Why* had she thought he'd be any different? He was the worst of them all. Taking a trip on an ego ride, pulling a woman he didn't actually *want*. Well, he'd won, hadn't he?

Only now she was humiliated. Now she had to get away. She hated her foolish naivety. She shouldn't have done it, shouldn't have trusted him. Shouldn't have thought she could ever have something easy and light in her life. Something just for herself. Shouldn't have thought, even for a second, that someone like him would…

On a gulp of horror she turned to rush away. But he

caught her from behind, stopping her headlong retreat, his arms like steel.

'Merle.'

A harsh, raw growl.

His heat, his thundering heart, pressed against her back briefly. Then he turned her around in his arms so it was her chest pressed to his. She bowed her head and closed her eyes for good measure. Not resisting his hold, not wanting to look in his eyes and see smugness, or rejection. Or, worse, anything like an apology. She would survive his mortifying explanation and then slink to her suite to wallow.

Ash stared down at her, furious with himself as confusion threw him into unaccustomed silence. Having her come to him like this was everything he'd wanted. He should've been kissing her already—glorying in the gorgeous silk of her body and celebrating the electricity that arced every time he got within ten feet of her.

Yet the second she'd said it, something felt wrong. Damned if he knew what or why. There was just a knot in his gut that had tightened to the point where he'd been unable to move. Until she'd started to run. Then he'd gone purely on instinct.

Now he couldn't let her go because her running away would be worse than anything. And, now he had his hands on her, he was unable to resist touching her more. But the tension in her body made him wary. His muscles felt prepped, ready to fight an internal war he didn't fully understand the reason for.

'You don't do this, Merle,' he said.

Was that it? Was that what was bothering him? Her

innocence? He growled beneath his breath as that spectre from his past flickered in his mind. The shy, innocent girl he'd humiliated and the horrific repercussions that had followed for him. 'I'm not going to be responsible for your broken heart.'

Merle stiffened and drew an audible breath. 'Of all the arrogant things to say,' she muttered. But she didn't pull free of his arms and she easily, easily could have. 'You're not going to break my heart. That's not what I want.'

'What do you want, then?' Ash glared at her as that strange fury within rose.

Her request had been so spartan, so dispassionate. She wanted him as if he were some kind of take-away option in a food court. It niggled. Even though it was exactly all he ever did.

'Don't panic,' she snapped. 'I'm not about to request your hand in marriage. I have that message loud and clear.'

He couldn't even pull together a grin. 'You—'

'Don't need rose petals or candles, or anything sappy like that.'

Her cynicism punctured his lungs. Her rejection of anything romantic made him feel worse. 'Nothing sappy?' He cupped her chin, making her look up so he could see into her eyes. 'So what, shall we just make a time to meet in your bed? A half-hour appointment or something?'

A wall of red scaled her face—a swirl of embarrassment and hurt. Finally she tried to twist away from him. 'Forget it—'

'No,' he said flatly. He refused to do that. Refused to

release her. But the second she stilled he softened his hold, treating her like the wild bird she was—fragile and flighty, a creature who needed freedom to feel safe. He couldn't resist caressing her gently, smoothing his hands down her back, tracing her beautiful shape. He wanted her in his bed—more than anything he'd wanted in a long time. But he didn't want it quite like this. Not so clinical and cold. Not when she made him feel anything *but* cold. Anything but himself. Hell, she made him feel as if he had to do the honourable thing.

And what's that? he mocked himself. To be protective? Chivalrous? Assume he knew better than she? What was he *thinking*? More importantly, what was *she* thinking?

'Don't you want more than this?' he growled. More than a night that meant nothing and would go nowhere?

'Are you asking that because I'm a virgin?' Her eyes sparked with that dangerous edge.

The word winded him, even when he'd known.

'Probably,' he admitted, helpless to be anything but honest in the intensity of her gaze. 'You don't strike me as reckless and you've held on to your virginity for a long time.'

He'd have had her yesterday if they'd stayed in that bunker, which was why he'd unlocked it. That one kiss had been incendiary. When she was in the vicinity his reasoning escaped him completely, but Merle Jordan wasn't a player on an equal footing to him. He had to remember that.

'What makes you think this is reckless?' she said. 'Perhaps I've taken the time to think it through.'

'It's barely more than twenty-four hours since we met.' He huffed out a tense breath.

'I bet you've slept with women you've barely known half an hour.'

He couldn't actually deny that. But *she* couldn't say the same. She was a thinker. Measured. Cautious and deliberate. So what had changed? He needed to know her *why*. 'Have you formulated a list of pros and cons?' he asked.

'Actually, yes, I have.'

He almost laughed. 'Tell me.'

Her shoulders tensed. She might be reliant on reticence, but she had courage when it counted. Even though he knew she was mortified, she summoned the strength to speak.

'On the negatives, it might be a little…uncomfortable.' She shot him an awkward look and her blush burned again. 'But your experience will be a good thing. One of us will know how to…what to…'

'Right,' he muttered, saving her from further stammering. 'Any other possible negatives?'

She bit on her lower lip. 'I have the feeling I might like it a lot.'

He nearly choked. 'That's a negative?'

'That kiss was…a revelation,' she said. 'Obviously. That's why I'm here now.'

An inordinate amount of pride flooded him because he knew her descriptor was an understatement. He was always considerate with a lover but never had it mattered as much. Never had he really *cared*. He wanted her to experience the absolute best.

'So the problem is I might want more than what you're able to offer,' she murmured.

More than what he was able to offer? In what way? He didn't want to know.

He had to move on. 'And the pros?'

'I'll finally get to experience what most other women my age have been enjoying for years.'

Desire held him in thrall, yet there was that irritation on the underside of his ribs. That resistance within him still. He didn't know why. It was a hitherto unawakened instinct, rapidly being overridden by another one— that usual hunt for hedonism. Why was he worried this might end in a mess? It'd only be a night like any other. But that whisper rose again, telling him that walking away now would be the right thing to do.

Right for whom?

A different, far louder whisper mocked. Because damned if Ash ever did the right thing. He was Hugh Castle's son, after all. He wasn't supposed to have a conscience.

'What if there's a worst-case scenario?' he growled. 'What if the contraception fails and you end up pregnant?'

'It's unlikely,' she said. 'You've managed not to get anyone pregnant before, right?'

'You've thought of everything.' Whereas he'd been consumed by pure lust. Barely able to think of anything else all day.

'But here's the biggest problem.' She put her hands on his chest as if to steady herself. 'I want more, remember?' She gulped. 'I don't want one night, I want *every* night that you're here.'

Every night? For the first time the prospect of more than one was undeniably arousing. Because this was Merle—shy, wary Merle, saying exactly what she wanted. And it was him.

A shocking possessiveness surged, shooting satisfaction through every muscle, but he couldn't move. Couldn't answer. It was the strangest sensation to be so transfixed. To be so tempted. To be so touched.

She gazed up at him—reading something in his face—and began to backpedal. 'You don't have to... you can just forget it. I'm sorry. You were probably just bored and—'

He kissed her. It was the only way to smash away her defensive barrier. It was the only thing he wanted. He could no longer resist the need howling inside him. Never had he been as conflicted about, as fascinated by someone.

But suddenly all that indecision inside was burned off by the far more important need to coax her sweet, sultry response. To his pleasure, it took the merest moment. With the softest of moans her soft, yielding body pressed against his. Satisfaction sluiced through him. He had no doubts now. He'd give her what she wanted. *All* that mattered was *her* satisfaction.

Merle couldn't catch her breath. She could feel his energy coil and passion build in his kisses. Her heart thundered as her doubts remained. He'd looked so surprised, so conflicted...she didn't want him doing this from pity. But as the dominance deepened in his kiss he held her with more assurance, more purpose. As if sensing her final concerns, he pressed her against the hard evidence of his arousal so she could make no mistake. He wanted her. His barely contained energy washed away the sting of rejection she'd felt only moments earlier.

'I have to go back on Sunday. So I will give you a week,' he promised slowly, his eyes glittering. 'But you have to give me time too.'

She frowned, still dizzy, not understanding.

'The *days*,' he clarified, possessively running his hand down her spine and pressing her more firmly against the steel wall of his body. 'You'll take the rest of the week off work and spend every moment with me.'

His request shocked her. While she wanted all the nights, somehow the days seemed more intimate. More intense. More terrifying.

'I have work to do.' She licked her dried lips.

'You worked all weekend.' He watched her intently from beneath lowered lids, his usual easy amusement veiled. 'I bet you're already ahead of your contractual obligations.'

'But—'

'Leo will be sued for flouting health and safety rules if you don't take days off like you're supposed to. He'll get done for providing an unsafe work environment. And Leo, I know, is a stickler for the rules.'

A flash of fear gripped her. He wanted *everything*. *Relax, fool. It'll just be a holiday fling.*

Wasn't that exactly what she wanted? All Ash was doing now was tweaking this new game. Raising the stakes, out to win what *he* wanted. The gleam in his eyes intensified, the curve of his sensual mouth deepened and he bent his head to brush his lips across her

cheekbone. And that was the point at which she sur-
rendered.

She could barely think for the way his fingers slid
over her, for the heat in his gaze as he studied her
mouth, for the way temptation was unfurling fronds
of anticipation from deep in her belly. She didn't know
why he'd hesitated before. Maybe she'd misread that—
her own doubt demons amplifying what had merely
been a moment of surprise. Honestly? It didn't matter
any more. Not when he was touching her like this.

She breathed out slowly. 'You want…'

'Your company.' His lips roved. 'All week. If this is
what you want, then we're going all in.'

All or nothing.

It was up to her whether to take it or leave it. That
was when she realised Ash Castle would always win,
whatever the game he was playing. He had that intense,
focused determination to make the play as perfect for
himself as he could. But Merle couldn't walk away from
what he could make her feel. She didn't want to. So she
finally uttered the one little word she'd been biting back
since the moment she had first set eyes on him.

'Yes.'

His lips met hers again—luscious kisses that were
intoxicating and everything she'd wanted. Yet the need
burning through her body wasn't soothed. Until with
infinite, terrible, wonderful slowness he unzipped her
coveralls.

'Merle…' He muttered so low, his words almost
slurred together '…do you have any idea how beautiful you are?'

'Don't—'

'Speak the truth?'

'Flatter me.' She closed her eyes as he caressed the skin he'd exposed.

'Is it so hard to believe I might be being honest?'

'Can't you just kiss me? We don't need to complicate—'

'Not complicate,' he corrected with a smile. 'Communicate. I want to know what you like, sweetheart. What you want. What you need. Be honest with me.'

She stared into his eyes—dazed, confused, aching. Hadn't she just been honest? Hadn't she just asked? She didn't know what else to say…

His hand swept across her shoulder and up her neck. His fingers splayed and he cupped the back of her head, holding her so he could see into her eyes, so he could lean so close she could feel his breath, so he could tease… But that burn within her was too strong. She glared at him.

'Okay.' He chuckled and, drawing her close, pressed his mouth to hers again.

Such a contrasting, delicious mix of hot and soft and hard and irresistible. She leaned into him as with sure, bold strokes he fanned the flames igniting inside her. Her yearning built as he created sensations she'd never experienced but wanted so much more of. Her toes curled as he nibbled her earlobes and then gently sucked them into soothing submission. It was the most shockingly erotic, intimate thing.

'Sweetheart.' His sigh was tense as she shuddered. 'You're making a mess of all my good intentions.'

'What intentions?' she breathed shakily.

'To do what I've been dreaming about for ever.' He toyed with the silky slip of a bra she wore.

She shook her head, unable to speak. But he'd not been dreaming about her for ever.

'Pleasing you,' he muttered. 'I ache to please you.'

His mouth was on hers again, so she couldn't answer, while his fingers had slid south and were wreaking havoc on her most secret places. Teasing, exploring and so infuriatingly, magically wicked, he brushed against the soft fabric of her panties and she was so glad she'd been too hot to bother with anything but her underwear beneath her coveralls today. The slide of his tongue in her mouth matched the slide of his fingers against her aching, hungry core. She moaned at the insistent, playful pleasure. Oh, he was big and strong and wicked. She clutched at his shoulders, barely able to stay upright, gasping as it suddenly sneaked up on her.

'Like *that*, Merle.' His rough growl of approval sent her over the edge.

'Ohhhhh.' An orgasm. *The* orgasm. So easy—from so little. But it was hard and quick and almost unbearable in its sudden impact and delight.

She closed her eyes, resting her head on his chest while she caught her breath. With her coveralls slipping from her shoulders and her legs trembling like those of a newborn deer, walking was impossible. Ash laughed delightedly and picked her up as if she were little more than a feather. Truthfully, she was a lot more.

'Seriously?' she half spluttered as he carried her inside and up the stairs to the second floor. She needed to provoke a little tease, to hear his voice so she could be reminded that this was just for fun. Just for now. 'You want to flex your superior strength?'

'Oh, I plan to flex everything, darling.'

Her little laugh faded as he placed her on the centre of his bed. She paid scant attention to the room or its stunning view across the bay. The view she couldn't ignore was right in front of her. The focus in his eyes ignited her senses even more.

He stood back and studied her supine on the bed before him, trying to suppress the desire to squirm her hips. His lips twitched. But then he glanced about, his energy almost crackling as he moved. She rose up onto her elbows to watch as he pressed a button and blinds closed out the rest of the world. He went into the en suite and returned a moment later with one of the gorgeously lush candles that were artfully placed everywhere.

'What are you doing?' she asked.

'Making it perfect.' He lit the candle and placed it on the table by the bed.

He didn't need candles to make it perfect. He just needed to touch her.

Amusement flickered in his eyes, dancing like the flame of the candle he'd just lit. 'You don't think you're worth going to any trouble for? Taking time for?' he teased very gently as he slowly removed her shoes. 'Because you couldn't be more wrong about that.'

She didn't know how to answer him. And then she simply couldn't, as with care and heat and wicked intent he slowly pulled the zip of her coveralls the rest of the way down to reveal her body to him.

He leaned over her and cupped the side of her face,

regarding her with impossible seriousness. 'If you don't value yourself, sweetheart, no one else will.'

'You sound like an inspirational social media meme,' she said in a small voice.

At that he laughed. 'You're so defensive. Don't be shy, Merle.'

Easy for him to say. But she was more than pliant, she was willing and helpful as he peeled her coveralls from her.

'Accept nothing less than you deserve,' he muttered. 'You should be satisfied every time you allow a man near you, that's the bottom line—the minimum of what you should get from your lover.'

She didn't want to think about being with someone else in the future.

He, too, suddenly looked serious. 'Your body is for savouring, for worshipping,' he muttered, and the lowest of growls escaped him. 'It's for me.'

The determination in his gaze, that glittering assurance of so much more, melted her.

'I'm going to kiss every inch of you, Merle.' It was half seeking permission, half savage promise.

She could barely nod, she could only enjoy as that tension swirling inside built. More than curiosity, more than yearning, it became hunger. Fierce, impatient hunger. Unclipping her bra, he tossed it to the side to leave her clad only in her plain black briefs. He returned to kissing her—teasing one tight nipple with his tongue while torturing the other with the tips of his too-clever fingers. Then he slowly pushed the panties down her legs, until she was completely bared. Despite that overwhelming heat, now there was vulnerability and her shyness returned. She'd never been naked in front of a man before. She wanted to pull up the sheet to cover her. But the only covering she received was Ash himself. He lay beside her, one leg across hers, his hand splayed across her stomach. His fingers loosely skittered over her skin, helping to ground her. Yet still rousing her. She looked into his eyes and knew what he wanted to do. And she wanted to let him.

With infinite patience he kissed her. Starting again. Melting away every one of those last inhibitions and shreds of self-consciousness. Slowly he kissed every speck of her skin, gently, hungrily working his way to her most private places. Until she was no longer shy, until she was aching for him to reach the destination that was now slick with anticipation for his touch. For his tongue. For the gorgeously wanton way she knew he'd make her feel. Where before she'd thought she wanted a sheet to cover her, now she didn't care. She was so hot, writhing in pursuit of more of the ecstasy he'd given her before. She was suffering such wicked delight beneath the ministrations of his hands and lips and teasing hot breath. But she trusted him with her body. With every intimacy.

He kissed her until she moaned, breathless and hot and aching in all those secret parts he'd stirred to life. Her hips lifted and his hands swept over them—heavy and sure, and kisses followed. Merle closed her eyes. Even the flickering candlelight was now too much to handle. All she could do was focus on the sensations as he licked and nibbled her with the most torturous slow rhythm that was utterly relentless, utterly rapacious. She gasped as the tension within—the tension he'd roused—finally snapped, tossing her once more into shuddering, fantastic ecstasy. Longer this time. Sharper. She had to scream through it.

He gently kissed her back to calmness. And then he pulled her past it to a place where she was restless again, where there was an ache, an unfinished sensation. This wasn't enough. Not yet.

He looked into her eyes and obviously saw the silent wish. He moved off the bed and shoved his swim shorts down. *Finally.* Even all those hours she'd seen him in little else had not prepared her for the impressive, erotic vision of him before her now. His skin was smooth and glittered slightly as the sheen of sweat caught the candlelight. That time beneath the sun had tanned him and it emphasised the fabulous bulges and dips of every hewn muscle. She began to tremble as her whole body ached with recognition and longing. He caught her gaze, held it—and her—transfixed. A half-smile curved and he returned to brace himself beside her on the bed.

'You're sure about this?' His fingers teased up her thigh.

If she hadn't been before she certainly was now. 'Yes. Please. So sure.'

He was as breathless as she and he held her with such reverence. As if there was nothing in the world he wanted more than this. Thoughtful, teasing deliberation preceded every touch. He was so damned careful, so responsive to her reactions. She shifted beneath him restlessly as he took his sweet, savage time to stir her all over again. She didn't want him to be *restrained*, determined to make it special for her because of her inexperience. He probably wasn't, of course. He'd be this considerate with any lover. Because it was the way he was. His innate courtesy lay beneath the teasing play-boy persona. He was multi-faceted—with depths he didn't usually like to display. That realisation peeled away something else within her. He'd bared more than just her body. He had her heart in his hands too. Suddenly she was so vulnerable, so exposed, so much more than physically.

He paused. 'You okay?' Somehow he'd sensed the shift within her. 'We can stop any time. If you change your mind...' He puffed out a difficult breath. 'Just say.' His whisper of reassurance was more of a groan.

His awareness, his concern, undid her even more.

'I don't want to stop. I don't want *you* to stop.' She wanted this more than she'd ever wanted anything. More than an ache. More than desperation. She shivered as that trust surged and the truth escaped. 'I just want you. As amazingly out of control as I feel.'

Something flared in his eyes. A satisfaction. A hunger. But then restraint swept in and his jaw clenched. 'Later.'

'*Now.*' A whispered, heartfelt command.

He stared into her eyes and she saw then his internal, then physical shift. Instinctively, she slid her legs further apart as he pressed close. She was so focused on him she forgot everything but what was happening in this moment. Ash with her. Ash holding her. Ash sliding inside her, finding his way into her tight-held confidence. He moved slowly, but with a heated strength and a powerful surety that made her shiver even as she welcomed his penetration. It was shockingly real, shockingly good as he gently rocked into her.

'Oh,' she groaned. She could hardly breathe. Hardly believe.

'Okay?' he muttered through clenched teeth. 'You need me to go slower?'

She shook her head and drew in a shuddering breath at the pleasure-pain, the overwhelming sensation, of his first possession. 'Don't stop.'

She wanted this. She liked this—she had the dawning feeling she was about to *love* this.

She sighed as he pushed deeper still, then ebbed, allowing her a chance to breathe. To adjust. And then he slowly pressed again—pushing closer to her. He smiled as she gasped again at the pure sensation. All she could do was curl around him, her hands sliding across his muscular back to find purchase and hold him closer still.

'Ash...' It was so sensational, she was so enraptured, she'd lost her speech.

His gorgeous smile quirked. 'Too gentle?'

It was a blissful, sweet torture. She wanted it exactly the same, yet he was right. She wanted a touch more. So gentle, so fierce, she felt so *full*. Somehow he worked his hand between them, teasing her to slipperiness to ease his occupation. Patience and confidence in his touch, in his relentless, claiming rhythm. It overpowered her again—sudden and hard. She convulsed in spasms of pleasure as the orgasm smashed through her. He growled as she came apart. She clutched him passionately, the fierce power and strength of her own body a surprise as she clamped about him, locking him inside her.

'Merle...' he breathed rawly, almost a warning.

Pressed deep into the mattress by his strong body,

she was breathless, almost broken, floating on a current of bliss even as aftershocks made her tremble. Yet he still hadn't had his release. The breathlessness she'd sensed in him before was under control now. Why was he so in control? Didn't he want to finish? Doubts rivered through her even as she felt the hard hunger of him still inside.

'Isn't this good for you?' she asked. She had to ask now. 'Ash—'

'Don't worry about me.' He rested his forehead on hers briefly, his eyes looming close but still so alert. Then a smile tore through his tense expression. 'Demanding woman, aren't you?'

'I just want you,' she said.

He was powerful and strong and she wanted him to be entirely *hers*. The way she'd just been *his*. He was so controlled—too controlled. But at her words that glint lit in his eyes. He lifted his head and pulled his hips back, only to surge close again—anchoring himself deep within her. Impossibly, excitement flowed again, firing her lax muscles into anticipation. Into movement. She rocked beneath him, provoking another fierce thrust from him. She held his gaze—proud, uninhibited. He was in her, with her, and he would give her what she wanted. Himself. That delicious sensation arrowed from her core out to every extremity, curling her muscles in the tight torture of bliss.

'Ash.' She could barely think of her words. 'I want you…'

She didn't know what to do with herself. She was so unprepared for the emotions tumbling through her. And he knew. In the triumph that flashed just before his self-control crumbled she saw his satisfaction. But then he moved—faster, harder, finally out of control, and his grip was tight and his intensity ferocious. His breath came short and quick to match hers as he thrust deeper and harder. And she loved it. She absolutely, hungrily, desperately loved it. She moaned, unrestrained, her response flying full and free, and she revelled as he groaned in reply. He talked, then, in a low growl, expressing the desire, the pleasure, the want, the sheer celebration of finally being right here. Like this. With her. In her. Again and again and again.

The words, the action, the kiss, the carnal completion pushed her to a place she'd never imagined. To a place where time stilled and sensation soared. She arched in a moment of sensual agony. And then devastatingly fierce fireworks exploded from the centre of her body, cascading in blinding brilliance. She screamed as she shook and then tears tumbled as the sensations overtook everything. She was torn to pieces by pure pleasure.

He cried out too. Growling her name with a desperate moan as he lost control in her arms.

But he didn't let her go. He held her. He stroked her hair back from her face, brushed away the few tears that she couldn't stop. They were of pleasure and wonder, gratitude and, okay, yes, with a whisper of sadness. Of not having known for so long that life could and should include *this*.

He kissed her gently as she slowly calmed. He caressed her carefully until the oversensitivity of her skin was soothed and she accepted the extent to which she'd just been irrevocably altered. Not just by having sex, but also by the joy of having someone treat her with passion and tenderness and with utter focus on her needs. Of being gifted an experience so profoundly intimate and pleasurable. One she would never regret, never forget.

And then he did it to her all over again.

CHAPTER SEVEN

'Do you never sleep in?'

Ash chuckled at Merle's drowsy question as he set a coffee beside her. He'd always had more energy than he knew what to do with.

'No lie-in *ever*?' She stifled another yawn.

'Drink this and get dressed—'

'Dressed?' She half pouted. 'Is that necessary?'

He paused to appreciate the glimpse of unguarded, luscious laziness. Quiet, primly hard-working Merle had melted into a warm, messy woman who'd whispered what she wanted and destroyed him.

'You're not tempting me back to bed with you,' he said firmly.

Actually, she totally was, but after last night he wanted to see if he could resist—even for a few minutes. He needed fresh air to clear his head and the warmth of the sun on his skin to bring back his energy. And he wanted to share that with her.

'I have plans.' He tempted her with a little mystery. 'Good ones, I promise.'

'You *promise*?' She eyed him with teasing amusement. 'That's big.'

'Not the only thing that's big.' He winked and walked out, chuckling at the groan that followed him.

Fifteen minutes later he smiled again at the sight of her. Back in the black coveralls, she had a hint of heat in her cheeks despite her teasing banter just before. She looked at him and their gazes meshed. Neither of them spoke, yet everything from the night before flickered in his mind. Her gaze suddenly slipped and she intently studied the basket on the kitchen counter as the colour in her cheeks rose. His heart missed a beat and for a moment that feeling returned—the hesitation, the confusion of whether this was the right thing.

Too late now.

He'd taken her—had his way with every inch of her body. Yet he'd not had his fill. Thank heaven he had the week to satisfy her. He'd thought it pure novelty, but now fierce determination flooded him, drowning that uncommon tendril of doubt that had sprouted again. He'd give her an affair she'd never forget.

She reached for the basket. 'We're going...'

'On an adventure.' He batted her hand away, not letting her see what he'd packed. 'You might want to bring a swimsuit.'

Her smile flashed back. 'You just want me out of my coveralls.'

'You just think I'm shallow.' He scooped up the basket and led her to the shed down by the water. 'Are you okay with boating?'

'Do we have to paddle?' She shot him a sideways look.

'No.' He laughed as he unlocked the door. 'We have a motor.'

'Oh, wow.' She stared at the classic motorboat that was stored pride of place in the shed. She fluttered her fingertips along the smooth, highly varnished wood as he opened the rear doors out onto the ramp. 'It's fabulous—we should be on the Italian riviera.' She looked at the other equipment stored in the big shed. 'You really do have all the toys.'

He glanced around the walls briefly before focusing back on the boat he'd not been out in for a decade. 'Most of it's new, but we've had this beauty for as long as I can remember. My mother bought it but I guess it was too valuable for my father to part with,' Ash muttered. 'Even when she was too unwell to walk, I'd carry her down for a spin on the water.'

'That must've been hard.'

'It was kind of normal.' He tried to pull together some perspective. 'There were good moments here.'

But there'd been bad moments too. And the last tainted all other memories of this house. Disappointing someone who really mattered, hurting them irreparably, was the worst. And he had to live with it for the rest of his life. He couldn't change it. Forgiveness could never be attained.

'Ash?'

At that soft query he reluctantly glanced over. The compassion in Merle's gaze had deepened. He didn't deserve it. 'Shall we see if it starts?' He turned away.

The engine coughed, then roared to life.

'First try.' She picked up the basket and came down to the end of the ramp. 'Does it go fast or is it just for show?' She shot him a look as she shrugged on the life jacket he handed to her.

That look was like a spark, bringing him back to the present. He smiled. 'It goes fast.'

Merle beamed. 'I expected nothing less.'

Onboard he let the engine go, whizzing them out along the coastline and past the next couple of bays. Then he headed inland. Merle curled cross-legged on the navy cushions, her face tilted towards the morning sun, her eyes closed. Ash realised almost too late he wasn't watching where he was steering. He cut the engine so he didn't crash them into the dock by accident. Merle blinked at their destination, directing a questioning look at him a second later.

'You must be hungry—you haven't had breakfast.' He stepped from the boat onto the dock.

'Isn't there food in the basket?'

'No. That has other essentials.' He tethered the boat securely.

'Surely it's too early for it to be open?'

Five stars and famous, the restaurant had a waiting list a mile long, so he couldn't quite understand Merle's audible reluctance. 'We're just picking up a package. It won't take a moment. Come on.'

Ash knew the owner and had phoned ahead to ensure they had what he needed. Up at the building, the door was open.

'Hey, Josie.' He gave the waiting woman a quick hug.

'It's been for ever, Ash.'

'It has,' he acknowledged briefly. 'Thank you for doing this.'

'Of course.' Josie smiled, not even trying to hide her curiosity. 'Are you staying long? What are your plans for the house?'

'I'm not sure yet.'

A total lie. He'd have an assistant finalise the sale as soon as he returned to Sydney. Interested buyers had been trying to contact him for months but he'd avoided their calls. Having seen the house now, understanding the changes, there was no question what he'd do. His heart seized and he instinctively turned, seeking his favourite distraction. Besides, he didn't want Merle thinking he didn't want to introduce her to Josie. But she'd vanished. Frowning, he looked more keenly for her and spotted a flash through the window. She'd disappeared into the shadows just outside to intently study some sign.

He thanked Josie again and hurried to catch Merle before she disappeared altogether.

'Why didn't you come in?' he asked as he walked her back to the boat.

'You didn't want anyone to know you were here. I imagined you wouldn't want to be seen with anyone else either.'

She didn't realise that he was pretty much always seen with someone—that it was more unusual for him to be alone in social spaces. Maybe her decision had nothing to do with him. Maybe she'd been playing safe, the way she always did around other people. And she said nothing more now. Did she not talk to people unless they spoke to her first? Did she always hide? Always only work? His curiosity escalated. Why was that? And why the hell was she *homeless*? She was intelligent and did a good job. What had gone wrong in her life for her to be as alone as she seemed to be?

As they chugged back out into the bay, he watched

her relax. He wanted to see her step out into the sunlight again. Her knew she liked the warmth of it. He thought she needed it. But he said nothing, knowing when to hold and when to play his hand. Fifteen minutes later, he slowed the boat and guided it to the small private bay that the outgoing tide had exposed.

She glanced back at him. 'Ash. This place is magical.'

Yes. It was the perfect place for the Merle he'd first met that night—the Merle who'd been in her element in her bath full of bubbles and beauty.

'It's actually still our property, but it's only accessible by boat and only at the right time with the tide.' He jumped into the water and held up his hand to help her down.

'So you timed this 'specially?'

He had.

'And this is your idea of breakfast?' Merle giggled as he unpacked the container Josie had handed to him. 'Champagne and oysters?'

He grinned. He'd known she'd appreciate it—and sharing this with her? This was fun. 'Aren't you going to have any?'

He'd poured the champagne and shucked four oysters already, and apparently all Merle could do was stare.

'I've never eaten them,' she confessed.

'Ever?'

She shook her head.

'Here's to another first, then.' Suddenly he had so many firsts in his head for her. He couldn't help teasing. 'You've heard they're an aphrodisiac?'

'Ash.' She glanced at him with those gorgeous eyes.

'I don't think I need an aphrodisiac. Right now I need something to calm me down and make me rational again.'

Her slightly husky, sassy honesty stopped his heart.

'But I like irrational Merle the best,' he countered.

'Is it hard to shuck them?' She watched him pull another shell from the container, chips of ice scattering onto the sand.

'No. I holidayed here every summer all my youth.' He laughed and passed her a half-shell. The plump oyster gleamed.

'You first,' she muttered, looking very doubtfully at the succulent blob.

He obliged, then raised his brows at her. She took the next one he held out and drew a breath. He watched as the salty treat disappeared between her sweet lips.

'Thoughts?' he asked when she'd swallowed.

'I'm…not sure.' Her nose wrinkled.

He laughed, again enjoying her honesty. 'Try another.'

She sipped her champagne to wash it down and Ash broke into the fresh-made fluffy bread and the twist of paper with home-churned butter that had also been in the parcel from the restaurant. She was *very* appreciative of that combination. He smiled, hiding the aching urge to kiss her, but he knew where that would lead and he still had that odd yearning to prove self-restraint to himself.

Merle finished her bread, licked her lips and suddenly stood.

'Are you going in the water?' he asked as she stepped across the sand.

She glanced back at him. 'I thought I would.'

'Not in those coveralls—you'll drown.'

'Then I'd better take it off.' A flicker of colour built in her cheeks. 'I need to clear my head.'

She had a simple black tee beneath and she slipped that over her head to reveal scarlet underwear. *Scarlet.* He sat back on his hands, tickled. She hadn't had the opportunity to go shopping in the last twenty-four hours, so those scarlet strips of silk weren't new, weren't bought specially for his benefit nor any other lover's. These were hers, bought for her *own* pleasure. The heat in his belly exploded. He liked that she indulged herself—those little individual puddings, the bubble bath, the scarlet silk. Her combination of inexperience and earthiness, of sensuality and hesitation with that occasional unpredictability fascinated him.

The urge to chase her was growing. His muscles tensed with the need to wrap her legs around his waist and hold her close. But this was more than his usual desire for release—more than a merely physical ache. This was more fun and more precious. He made himself remain still and watch—appreciating her full, gorgeous curves and inner effervescence as she giggled at the temperature of the water. He only lasted ten seconds before he threw aside any stupid thoughts of self-restraint. He only had a week and it suddenly felt like nothing. He quickly pulled what he needed from the basket and stripped off.

Moments later, he dived after her like the shark he was. He wound his arm around her waist, and to his infinite satisfaction she curled her arms around his neck. Kissing her was pure pleasure. He couldn't deny her.

Couldn't deny himself. Even after last night, he wanted her more. She'd unlocked a vault of hunger in him. He carried her out of the water and set her down.

'This is a gorgeous rug,' she practically purred.

'Essential,' he breathed.

He'd tossed it down in those frantic seconds before joining her in the water. Because he didn't want her sand-burned, didn't want her soft skin marked in any way. He rolled onto his back so she was above him. Time stretched. A treasure trove of possibility spread over him. He peeled away the scarlet to bare her breasts. She was stunning and he could hardly stand it as she swept her hands, her mouth, her body over his. This was a woman lost in the throes of desire, exploring her sensuality with him. And he'd never felt as lucky. It felt like a first time for him too—this discovery.

'Like that?' she asked, a breathless sweet echo of his own check-in with her last night. Ensuring understanding, acceptance, pleasure.

The blue sky was a background to her beauty. Brilliant, almost blinding, the whole world seemed hot and vital. She writhed above him—with a moan, with a choked laugh. His heart beat painfully. She killed him. Never had he experienced such sweet, heady enjoyment. She was fresh and intoxicating and wicked. She didn't offer the slick moves of a lover aiming to please another. This was too innocent, the expression in her eyes too dazed. Joining her in this was a privilege that he could only strive to deserve—vowing to make it better for her still. She groaned as he worked his hand between them, feeling her flaring response—and his own complete unravelling.

'You're stunning.' And he was helpless. Unable to think of anything more intelligent to say as she made him arch and shout, 'Merle!'

'I didn't think it could get better than last night.' Merle drowsily studied Ash but couldn't get a read on what he was thinking. He sipped his drink, gazing across the water, his breathing taking time to slow. And as she too slowly recovered, she began to imagine the full extent of the week's possibilities.

He glanced down and met her gaze, his mouth quirking. 'You look like a satisfied kitten.'

'Kitten?' she echoed with mock outrage. She did not want to be a *kitten*. 'Can't I be a panther?'

He answered with another bitingly gentle kiss and suddenly she was all out of shy patience. She didn't want more games. She just wanted *him*. She broke free from his gorgeously decadent lips and breathlessly asked him to take total advantage of her again.

'You've gone to so much trouble,' she muttered as she pulled the soft blanket higher up her shoulders another half-hour later.

'I really haven't,' he laughed lazily.

Perhaps for him it wasn't a bother. Perhaps all these things that were luxuries for her, were simply normal to him.

'Well…' she smiled a little sadly '…I appreciate it, so thank you anyway.'

He turned that intense gaze of his back on her and she saw questions in his eyes.

'Talk to me,' he muttered. 'Tell me everything.'

She shook her head. 'I'm pretty boring, Ash.'

'No. You're an enigma.'

'As flattering as that is…' She shuffled lower in the rug he'd cocooned about them. 'You're in for disappointment.'

'You're not used to talking about yourself?'

'Not used to someone being interested.' She laughed to let him know she was joking. Except they both knew it wasn't a joke. It was a sad, self-piteous truth that she instantly regretted uttering.

'Let me in, just a little.' An Ash Castle dare.

She met his gaze. 'Will you do the same in return?'

'Sure.'

She laughed for real then. 'Are we really going to play emotional strip poker?'

'I'm asking for history, not emotion.'

'You don't think they go together?'

'No. There are just facts. Points along the way.'

'Points that move and shape you.'

He rolled his eyes. 'Why not show me just *one* of the cards you hold so close, Merle?'

She'd let him in—literally—so this shouldn't be difficult. And she wanted him to reciprocate because she wanted to understand what drove him to be as determined—as resolute—as he was. And as recklessly, relentlessly unattached. That he was obviously as curious about her? That tilted the balance. Was fascination as mutual as the desire between them?

'Come on,' he tempted. 'Where did you grow up? When did you get your first coveralls? Why did you go into archival work? I want the whole—'

'Biography? Really?' She tugged the rug higher. She

didn't want to tell him about her past. She didn't want him to pity her. Although she had the horrible suspicion he already did.

'Absolutely.' He leaned back and surveyed her, humour dancing with curiosity in his eyes. 'Why not start with the coveralls?'

'You can't cope with them, can you?'

'I've already told you I changed my mind about them.' Ash laughed.

And every time Ash laughed, Merle found herself slipping further under his spell.

'How and why did they become your go-to style?' He was like a terrier.

She sighed and relented. 'When I went to live with my grandfather I picked up a pair from his workshop and they were comfortable. I felt like I could do anything I liked in them.'

Ash leaned closer. 'There are so many things to unpick in that, I don't know which question to start with.'

She rolled her eyes but tightened her hold on the rug at the same time.

'Your grandfather,' he decided swiftly. 'When and why did you go to live with him?'

Merle gave in. There was no reason to hide this from him and telling him about it suddenly seemed easy. 'My mother was a back-up singer for a series of bands. She spent most of her time on the road, gigging here and there. It was hand-to-mouth and hard but she loved the lifestyle.'

He toyed with the edge of the rug near her fist. 'But how did you fit in with that lifestyle?'

'For the first decade I waited backstage. When I was

very small others in the band would watch me and as I got older I quickly learned to be quiet and stay out of the way. Half the time the headline artists didn't even know I was there. That's how I liked it and how she kept me safe.'

'Safe?'

'She worked late nights at downmarket venues. It was good to be invisible when I was a young girl.'

His frown set her on the defensive.

'Don't disapprove,' she said. 'Mum was amazing. She took great care of me. She taught me how to take care of myself.' Merle had known their situation was precarious and that she had to stay silent and good. 'She wasn't supposed to have me there, but she didn't want to leave me with strangers. I sat on a stool in the wings and read. She could see me from the stage. We were okay.'

'Then what happened?'

'When I was about twelve, she sent me to live with my grandparents. She said I needed to go to school, that I was too bright to be held back by her lifestyle. She wanted more for me.'

Ash's expression remained serious. 'Did you know your grandparents before you went to live with them?'

'My mother was young when she had me.' Heat built in her cheeks. 'Very young. They didn't want her to keep me. In the end she left home before I was born. They didn't approve of her choices but she was hard-working and she did everything she could to give me the best.'

'Did they approve of you? Of your choices?'

'Well…' She half smiled. 'My grandmother was determined I wouldn't make the same choices my mother had.' She'd lectured Merle about her mother's 'downfall' so many times. She'd been so controlling, so strict. But Merle had swallowed back the rebellion and resentment and she'd stayed silent. Knowing again that she had to, to survive.

'How did that determination play out?'

Merle's smiled twisted sadly. Ash was too astute—honing in on the most vulnerable angles in her answers.

'She could yell. A lot. It was best to be quiet. Fortunately I was good at that.'

Be silent, be good, be as unseen as possible. Even though she'd hated having to do so. Hated not being able to stand up for her mother. The one time she'd spoken up, she'd suffered a horrible slap-down. Literally. A punishment that had gone on far in excess of what her 'crime' had deserved. But now she shrugged the worst memories off.

'She lectured for hours. She wanted to control my every minute. So I tried to stay out of her way, out of sight really. I tried not to cause any trouble and not give her anything to be disappointed about.'

Her grandmother hadn't realised how hellish school was for Merle—there was no danger of her falling in with a 'bad crowd', because no crowd was interested in Merle.

Ash's frown didn't lessen at all. 'Where was your grandfather?'

'Out in the garage. He was a second-hand goods trader and he had a garage and shed full of everything you could possibly imagine. The safest, easiest way to avoid my grandmother was to be with him. I went with him to all the markets.' He'd given her safe haven from her grandmother. And from school.

'But he didn't stop your grandmother from shouting at you?'

'He did by taking me with him,' Merle countered. 'And when I was home I studied in my room. I did chores without question.' She looked at him and saw he still didn't understand. 'She wasn't well,' she whispered.

'So you had to be quiet and out of sight your entire childhood,' he said grimly.

It hurt, even though it was true. 'You're awfully good at judging.'

'Maybe.' He leaned over and looked into her eyes. 'You're awfully good at making excuses for all three of them.'

Her heart stuttered. 'They were the only family I had,' she answered simply.

'That I do understand.' His lips twisted in a gentle smile. 'So they *were*? What happened?'

She'd known he was going to ask but it was still hard to articulate. Her voice would hardly work. 'When Mum was on tour in Australia there was a fire at the lodge. They didn't have batteries in the fire alarms and they didn't have an up-to-date guest list. She died of smoke inhalation before they realised she was still in the building.'

She knew Ash was looking at her but she couldn't meet his eyes. She never spoke about this. Most of the time she tried not to even remember it.

'I'm sorry, Merle.'

She nodded mutely, her throat too tight for sound to emerge.

'You could've been there too,' he said softly.

She coughed. 'I know.' She'd stayed at that same lodge several times before the move to her grandparents'. 'I was a light sleeper as a kid,' she whispered. 'Maybe if I'd been there I would've heard something, maybe I'd have woken. Maybe I could have saved her.' She dreamed she had sometimes. Then she'd wake and remember the worst was real.

For a moment there was silence. But it wasn't strained, it was oddly connecting.

'I was devastated when my mother died,' Ash said gruffly, looking out across the water. 'Even though I knew it was coming, it wrecked me.'

His quiet admission devastated something within Merle.

'She had a heart condition all of her life,' he said. 'I always wished I could've done something about it even when I knew I couldn't.'

Merle's heart ached at the guilt echoing in his voice.

So he was human. He wasn't always supremely confident, floating through life with bulletproof, brilliant ease. He had hurts too. She'd known that. And whatever had happened with his father had cemented his slide into rebellion. It wasn't that he didn't care. Maybe it was because he cared an awful lot? And he didn't want to.

'How old were you?' she asked.

'Eighteen, at the end of my final year of school.' He frowned and looked back at her, that alert curiosity lighting his eyes once more. 'How was school for you—when you finally went?'

'Horrendous. I was never going to be popular like you.' She laughed a little sadly. 'And don't even try to tell me you weren't. People can't cope with someone being a bit different and I was *very* different. I'd never been to school, I had no clue how to play the social clique game...' She broke off.

'So how did you survive?'

'The same way as always. Stay quiet. Stay unseen. Sometimes it's better not to be noticed.'

'Merle—'

'Most of the time I succeeded,' she interrupted before he could contradict her.

It was easy to be invisible. Easy to avoid eye contact. Easy to avoid answering calls and replying to emails. Easy to be forgotten about.

'Most of the time?'

He'd heard the wistful edge of regret that she'd been unable to mask. But she didn't want to go there. Too embarrassing. There was a long moment of silence that she refused to break.

'Where are your grandparents now?' He didn't relent.

She sighed. 'Three years after I went to live with them, my grandmother had a stroke. She became more difficult. It was a hard couple of years before she had another stroke that left my grandfather on his own with me. He was worn out from caring for her and it took me a while to realise his cognitive abilities were declining. In the end, I couldn't manage him on my own, not with needing to work as well to support us both. So he went into a facility. I sold the house, and everything else, to ensure he got good care. He passed away eight months ago.'

'That's why you're between residences? You sold the house to cover his care costs?'

She nodded. 'I only got this job because my boss at the records management company is pregnant and needed someone who could take a live-in job. I did an interview online with Leo. I was lucky and I need to do a good job here.'

A flash of guilt curdled her blood. What was she doing taking the week off work? Worse—spending it with Ash like this? Fraternising with her client's half-brother was surely a huge mistake—the most unprofessional thing she'd done in her life.

'Don't panic.' He read her mind. 'I'm gone at the end of the week, remember? There won't be any repercussions. You'll get the job done. What's happened between us won't have any impact on the future.'

Wouldn't it? That seemed impossible. She wasn't the same person she was yesterday, was she? Or perhaps this wanton lover had been inside her all along, just waiting for Merle to allow that part of herself to be unleashed. There was no locking her away again now.

'That's why I'm not going to "burn the lot" like you keep telling me to,' she said softly.

'The only reason *I* haven't is out of respect for the volunteer firefighters.' He grimaced.

'You don't want to keep any of it?' She didn't quite understand why. 'You have good memories here.'

'I have bad ones too.'

She hesitated but had to ask. 'Did she die here?'

He nodded slowly. 'But I wasn't here at the time.'

He didn't want to talk about it. She recognised the reluctance because it mirrored her own. Digging too deep hurt. This week with him was only an interlude, an experience. One she had to handle *lightly*.

She threw the blanket off and stood up on the sand, shaking free of the melancholy that had briefly descended. 'I think it's time for another swim.'

CHAPTER EIGHT

ASH SAT ON the deck absorbing the morning sun and reading while waiting for her to wake. He'd swum, then prepped a simple breakfast that was on the table beside him. Letting her rest was hard. The selfish part of him wanted to go in there and wake her. But she needed her sleep; they'd shared yet another very late night.

He couldn't concentrate on his book. Memories stirred and impatience tightened his muscles. He hadn't holidayed in years. For all the nights out or weekends partying on a yacht, there'd always been a laptop on the desk, a call to be made, business to be done. But he hadn't checked his emails in four days—the longest stretch ever. Time had slipped easily and deliciously like those plump oysters had slid down his throat two days ago. Hours could be lost in the simple pleasure of kissing Merle Jordan and long, sunny days had bled into long, hot nights. It was easy to forget why he'd come here in the first place and that he'd never intended to linger like this. He focused only on Merle. Together, they'd discovered she had a penchant for skinny dipping and she'd laughingly embraced her sensual, hedonistic side. She also had a hidden decadence that was

dangerous to his peace of mind. They laughed, ate and
drank and duelled over anything and everything light
and simple. Drawing her out, engaging her, was reward-
ing. She was a quick learner and fiercely competitive
and now she held nothing back. Her teasing smile alone
sent anticipation rippling down his spine.

She'd blossomed before his eyes. But even though
she'd let him in, he was more curious than ever. She'd
been lonely, her early life lacking in laughter. He'd had
to teach her the rules to the most common of board
games. *That* was why she'd been so quick to choose
snakes and ladders the other night. It was the only game
she'd known how to play. He wanted her to experience
more of the things she'd missed out on. And he wanted
her to experience them with *him*.

Half an hour later she joined him, her eyebrows lifting.
'You wear glasses.'

'I do.'

'So there's *something* less than perfect about your
body,' she teased.

'You think the rest of my body is perfect?' He
smirked.

'It's not like you don't already know that.'

'Still, I'm touched, given it's *you* who thinks so.'

'My opinion matters?' Half disbelieving, half flirt.
Wholly gorgeous.

'Very much.'

She rolled her eyes and angled her head to read the
spine of the book he was holding. 'It's an amazing library in there. Someone took time and effort to amass
a good collection.'

'My father bought someone else's lifetime effort. He didn't carefully select each item himself. It was an investment,' he said drily. 'Like the art and the wine. It was for money, not love.'

'He loved the actual *collecting*.'

'He was avaricious. *Not* for love but for show. There's a difference.' Merle, Ash suspected, would always collect things for love. Things that held meaning to her. 'I still can't believe you don't have piles of dusty old things perfectly arranged in boxes with ridiculously detailed labels, keeping everything for ever and ever.'

She giggled and picked up the small bowl of fresh fruit he'd sliced for her. 'You think I'm a future hoarder?'

'Yes.'

She shook her head. 'Most of my mother's things were lost in the fire and her parents didn't keep any of her childhood things, so…' She shrugged. 'I guess that's why I went into archive work. Because I know what it's like to lose everything. I know that some things are irreplaceable.'

Her smile twisted when he failed to hide his sceptical expression.

'I watched my grandfather lose his memory,' she said. 'Maybe that's why it's important to me to help people hold memories for another. I think sometimes that's all we can do.'

'You don't think sometimes people hold on to things for too long? Everything eventually wears out as things rot or break—either way, they're rendered useless. Don't they just become a burden?'

'You don't have to keep hold of everything, Ash. You get to choose. Keep what matters and let go of the rest.'

He rested his head back against the chair. 'You make it sound easy.'

'You treasure these games now you've found them again,' she pointed out. 'You wouldn't part with them now.'

She was right, of course. Aside from Merle herself, they were the best thing about coming back. His mother was the reason he'd stayed away so long, but she was also the reason he'd returned now. He'd needed to see the place one last time. To say goodbye. For all of his teasing, Merle's words had an effect on him and he found himself seeing things from her point of view. There ought to be more here than those games of his mum's. There should be her personal papers and effects. The things he should have taken care of so much sooner.

'You really don't have anything of your own you treasure?' he asked. Surely someone who put sentimental value on things had *something* she prized?

'I once had a gorgeous copy of *Jane Eyre*. I got it at one of the car boot sales I went to with my grandfather.' Reminiscence softened and warmed her brown eyes. 'It wasn't exactly a first edition but it was old and lovely and had the nicest inscription.'

Ash frowned, confused. 'The inscription was from your grandfather?'

'No, *I* bought the book. The inscription was to someone else—the previous owner, I guess.'

She'd treasured a book that had been gifted to someone *else*?

'I know it sounds weird.' She laughed sheepishly at the look on his face. 'But it had obviously been treasured; it was in such perfect condition and it had been gifted with love. I didn't think it should just be thrown away.'

'You think the book itself was imbued with importance?'

'For me, yes. It deserved to be treasured—for itself, for the care between the two people. It shouldn't have been forgotten.'

'You don't think it stayed perfect because no one picked it up? Maybe it was put on a shelf and ignored for decades?'

'Why do you need to destroy my dreams?' She shot him a baleful look. 'Why can't I believe?'

He felt bad for suggesting it—but he doubted that the pristine condition of her book meant it must have been treasured. He'd long ago discovered that perfect facades, perfect stories, often hid horrible lies. But Merle still believed in generosity and sincerity, in humanity and kindness. *She* was genuine. And she believed in the gift of love from one person to another, even though she'd been neither a giver nor a recipient of much herself. For all of her self-protective measures, she was a romantic. And that tendril of doubt, of hesitation, turned to a touch of remorse.

'Did you like the actual story?' he teased. 'Did you even read it?'

'Of course I read it and I loved it.' She tilted her chin defiantly. 'Jane had a tough time, but she was strong and true to herself.'

'So you still have it?'

She nibbled her lip and put the bowl down on the table. 'I took it everywhere with me. I was sixteen and okay, yes, I was idealistic. It was just Grandad and me and I guess I was lonely and it became like a talisman of something...'

Of hope? Ash couldn't speak for the sudden ache in his chest. Concern for her grew, because he knew too well that things rotted and relationships were ripped away. *That* was reality. So something bad had happened to her lovely book. 'What happened?'

'I got a little lonely and made a fool of myself with a guy in my class. He started paying attention, acting as if...'

Ash tensed as she shrugged sheepishly. He had the horrible feeling he knew where this was going.

'I was gullible.' She confirmed the basis for his anxiety. 'I was easy pickings for a guy like him.'

'Like him?'

'Good-looking, popular...he had everything.' She frowned. 'Though I know he probably didn't, no one has everything all of the time.'

'Not even us privileged rich boys?'

Her smile quirked. 'He was curious about my book. I didn't realise people had noticed that I always had it. That they wondered about it. I was just oblivious to all that. He asked to borrow it. I'd inspired him to read it, apparently. I was flattered and I didn't want to deny him. Maybe he didn't realise how precious it was to me.'

'Don't let him off lightly, Merle,' Ash muttered. 'He knew.'

And Ash knew how it was to be young and thoughtless.

'Yeah. They all did.' She looked at him sadly. 'There was a clique, you know? I asked for it back days later. He laughed even as he said sorry. He said he'd lost it.

He'd put it in his sports bag and it must have fallen out or something.'

'You don't believe him?'

She shook her head. 'I think they just wanted to know what it was and why I always had it. Maybe they thought it might've been a secret diary and they wanted to mock my innermost thoughts. Maybe they were just mean.'

It hadn't been a precious diary, but it had mattered as much. She'd cared about it.

She'd given the idiot something that was precious to her and he'd trampled it—crushing her fledgling trust in the process. And she'd scuttled back into her corner, hiding in the shadows and attempting that damned invisibility.

'It was the deceit that got to me.'

Ash's chest tightened. *He'd* been deceitful. He'd cheated. And he'd hated how bad he felt for it. 'I won't lie to you, Merle.'

'I know. You value honesty.' She glanced at him sombrely. 'Someone lied to you.'

'Yes.' That was true. Yet he felt as if he was letting her down by not being completely honest now. 'But I've lied too,' he added. 'I was just like that jerk. When I was that age I was awful.'

'What did you do?'

'I cheated.'

Her eyebrows lifted. 'You were in a relationship at that age?'

It had hardly been a relationship. 'She wanted more than what I could give her and I was a coward.'

Merle paled. 'But you've learned your lesson?'

'Oh, yes, I've never done it again. Never will.'

She nodded slowly.

Amazed, Ash stared at her. She'd just accepted his word? She was too forgiving of shabby treatment. Too generous. But his mistake couldn't be forgiven by the one person who mattered most. It wasn't Rose—his 'girlfriend'—who'd suffered the most, though her humiliation had been total. It was his mother who he'd destroyed with his selfish carelessness. The truth he'd discovered then was that he was *less*. He didn't have Merle's depth of compassion. He didn't have her ability to hold someone's precious feelings—not their heart. He never had, never would. Because he was his father's son.

Normally he didn't think about it. He lived in the moment, lived by the rules he'd designed to keep everyone else safe. Because he'd learned who and what he truly was and he wasn't hurting anyone else again. Merle would be okay. She knew this was only for these few days. He'd made sure she understood. But he couldn't resist his own curiosity about her—couldn't help wishing he could make things better for her.

'So was that the guy you meant when you mentioned you'd said yes once?' he asked. 'That was secondary school, Merle. There must've been something since.'

'No one's asked again.'

'Maybe because you hide and avoid any situation in which that might become possible,' he suggested softly.

'Maybe because I've been busy,' she said defensively. 'I was looking after my grandfather, I was studying… and struggling financially, so I worked as well. There hasn't been the time for fun.'

She was right and he was an idiot for assuming she'd have had the time to be as frivolous as him.

'There's time now,' he said.

'Yes.' She lifted her head. 'There is now. With you.'

And she was embracing it. Except being here with him was still within her safe boundaries. This was her with him, but still hidden. He wanted her to have more. And yes, *he* wanted to have more too.

'Let's go out,' he said suddenly. 'Dinner and dancing.'

She looked startled. 'You mean like a date?'

'Yeah, why not?' He smothered his smile as he saw her hesitation. He bet there was a pro and con list leaping into her mind.

'You really struggle to do nothing and relax,' she said.

He laughed. 'You really struggle to be seen. And to have fun. You ought to go out.'

'So I know what to do for next time?' she asked.

A cold ball clenched in his stomach. 'So I get the pleasure of doing it with you first,' he said huskily. 'I want more of your firsts.'

Her eyes widened. For a moment he'd rendered her speechless.

Then she swallowed. 'What kind of dancing?'

'Any kind you want.'

She sank a little lower in her seat. 'I don't understand the appeal, to be honest.'

'Of going out dancing?'

'I saw the patrons at the clubs mum performed at and they were just... I don't know. Were they having a good time?'

'Have you never gone dancing yourself?'

'I haven't been in a club since I was a kid.'

'Your mother warned you off?'

'Sometimes the guy lingering around the stage door thought the back-up singers might be available for other services if their offer was enticing enough. Then my grandmother was all, *don't make a mistake like your mother. Sex is bad and shameful and men are dangerous. You're too young…*' She laughed bitterly. 'What chance did I have, really?' She tossed her head. 'But I'm not too young now. I know they both had baggage. I don't have to carry it for them. Sex can be fun and feel good and doesn't need to be over-complicated or over-emotional, right?'

The problem was this didn't feel all that *uncomplicated* to him. This was the most complex relationship he'd had with anyone—in years. And yet in some ways it was the easiest.

'We're definitely going on a date,' he said.

'We definitely don't need to do that,' she said, but then an alarmed look crossed her face. 'Are you bored?'

'Of course not.'

She didn't relax. If anything, she looked more concerned. 'I don't want you doing this because—'

'There's a difference between pity and simply sharing an experience with someone,' he interrupted her.

She narrowed her eyes. 'You wanted quiet and solitude.'

'I'm talking one night, Merle.'

'Always it's "one night" with you.' She pulled a face. 'But we've been on a date—when we went boating the other day.'

'Not the same thing. We'll fly to Auckland. Have dinner and stay the night. We'll return early the next morning.'

She still didn't say yes.

'Have you ever dined at an award-winning restaurant?' he cajoled. 'One with a live band?'

'As opposed to a dead one?'

'Ha-ha.'

'If it's so amazing, how are you going to get a booking at such short notice?'

He just smiled at her.

'Really?' She folded her arms across her chest and raised her brows. 'Money talks?'

'Generally speaking, yes.'

'Yet you couldn't find alternative accommodation for me so easily the other night, for all your money.'

'True,' he acknowledged. 'But you have to admit that's ended up working in my favour.'

He was ridiculously pleased to see she still blushed.

But she tilted her chin. 'Not even you can wear swimming shorts to dinner.'

'I'll have a suit delivered to the hotel.'

He suppressed his amusement at the stunned expression that flitted across her face. Then her expression fell. Her next worry was already evident.

'You want me to wear coveralls to a fancy restaurant?'

'You can wear whatever you want,' he answered easily. 'I'll find you as delectable as ever.'

She gazed at him and sighed, almost sadly. 'You do it so easily, you're not even aware of it.'

'Do what?'

'Seduce me into saying yes.'

CHAPTER NINE

ASH LEANED BACK against the table, drumming his fingertips on the wood behind him and debating whether he ought to knock on the door and ask if she was okay. She'd been locked in the bedroom of their hotel suite for over an hour. Was she worrying? Was she literally hiding again? *He* felt uneasy and he *never* felt uneasy. But she'd been taking too long. He straightened up, deciding to go, and then the door opened. Adrenaline blasted, stopping him dead. He was only able to stare.

'What are you wearing?' he croaked.

He'd not meant to say that. Not meant to question her choices or sound judgmental and make her self-conscious. But her smile flashed. Not just any smile— brilliant, unguarded, a tiny bit self-satisfied—so he knew she'd not taken his moronic question any of those wrong ways. She'd heard the underlying truth—he was stunned and too caught up in staring at her to care.

'I like how it feels,' she said.

Anticipation tightened every muscle. His beautiful secret sensualist was wearing a jumpsuit unlike anything he'd ever seen. A week ago he'd never have thought he'd find any kind of coveralls sexy, yet here it was happening again. But these weren't for protective purpose. They were scarlet and silk and sleeveless, and skimmed her body, clinging to the fullest points of her curves. The deep vee drew his eye and the fabric flowed as she walked towards him—in scarlet high heels to match. She'd left her hair loose so it hung down her back in a rich brunette swathe. Impossibly, her skin was even more radiant. She'd look less visible in a little black dress that revealed far more skin. This was so much better than that. This was Merle doing her thing, her way. The smile in her eyes felled him all over again.

'Are you okay?' she asked.

'I don't think so.' He groaned, literally backing away from her. 'We'd better go.'

He barely noticed the restaurant, barely tasted the food, was barely aware of the service or of anyone else present. He could only see her. He didn't know how he kept up with her banter. It was as if his brain had been stupefied.

'Will you dance with me?' he asked, unable to sit still a second longer.

For the first time all evening doubt shadowed her eyes. 'It might be more stand and sway than spin, okay?'

Stand and sway sounded perfect. He ached to get his hands on her—to anchor himself, to ensure she was real. As they walked towards that darkened area, he was aware of heads turning. Of course people looked—she was stunning. But it hauled up other concerns. While he wanted the world to appreciate her, he also wanted to keep her to himself. Suddenly he felt possessive.

Even here in Auckland he was recognisable. The

media in Australia had followed him for years. When he'd first turned his back on his father he'd welcomed the stupid society gossip blogs, annual most-eligible lists, relentless speculation and stories, all fuel to which he was the flame, to shame his father. But he didn't want Merle exposed to any negativity. If people found out what he'd been up to this week? It could totally be construed as a scandal. He'd seduced an innocent. Kept her in his holiday home to be his lover. It sounded as bad and mad as if he'd locked her in that damn bunker.

Wasn't it worse than humiliating Rose? Never had he been as selfish. But Merle was an adult—she'd *asked*. She'd wanted and she'd taken. This was a scandal they'd *both* desired and they were both determined to make the most of. But he couldn't help pointing out the problem to her.

'People are watching,' he muttered. 'Are you okay with that?'

'Oh, I'm fine.' She grinned. 'They're watching *you*.'

They were not.

'Okay—' she shot him a sideways look, together with an impish grin '—they're looking at me too. But I don't mind.'

He'd wanted to spoil her. He'd wanted her to have a night where the spotlight was on and she could see she could do more than survive in its light. He'd wanted to see and feel the world through her perspective some more because that hope, that optimism she had, was tantalising when he'd lost his so long ago.

'If you'd had cameras in your face all the time, trust me, you'd start to mind,' he muttered.

* * *

'Maybe.' Merle nodded.

Right now she didn't really care about anything—she was too busy basking in the glow of Ash's attention. How he'd worked out that people were watching them she didn't know because he'd not taken his eyes off her and it was thrilling. But it was more than his attention: it was his influence and his outrageousness that encouraged her own sense of liberation. He'd bluntly pointed out her right to speak up. That he lived and moved with such confidence inspired her to answer back, to be as blunt and as honest.

It wasn't that she didn't care about consequences, of course she did, but she wasn't afraid of them in the way she had been for half her life. She felt alive, as if she had vitality and fight within her to stand not just beside him but also in front of him and be bold. It was invigorating. Enriching. Addictive. She spread her hand across his chest, feeling his tension, the powerful thump of his heart against her palm. Ash did not stay still. He was full of vigour and vitality and humour. He had more energy than anyone she'd ever met—a freewheeling force of nature. But he'd been so careful with her. Tender. He'd channelled all that energy, focused it on her pleasure. There was nothing as seductive as all of his attention.

She'd not realised how stuck she'd become. How constrained. Why had she let things hold her back for so long? She'd not wanted to see the problematic issues from her upbringing but perhaps he'd been right about that too—that she'd made too many excuses for too long, ignoring the impact on herself. She loved her family and she knew they'd done their best but it hadn't been easy for her—she'd not been the priority. But now she had absolute freedom and she could live her own life on her own terms. And she wanted to.

'What are you thinking?' Ash suddenly asked.

She glanced up at him and smiled.

His hold on her tightened. 'You're more luminous than ever.'

She laughed. 'It's the lighting in here.'

'No.' The question in his beautiful amber eyes was unrelenting. 'Tell me what you're thinking.'

How could she resist him anything when he looked at her like that?

'That I'm happy.' She blinked back a sudden burn behind her eyes. 'I'm enjoying the freedom to do what I want. How I want. When and where and with whom I choose.'

And that was with Ash.

She felt the response ripple down his body. He wasn't perfect, but he didn't claim to be. He'd been honest—letting her know he had flaws and had made mistakes. And he'd made her appreciate that other people in her life hadn't been perfect either. Despite her tendency to try to see the best, sometimes it was good to accept an honest assessment.

And honestly? She adored her new jumpsuit. She'd searched online and had it delivered direct to the hotel—living like Ash Castle himself. It had arrived on time and hadn't even needed alterations. It was comfortable yet sexy and she didn't regret blowing some of her pay on it. It had been so long since she'd done something for herself.

Aren't you doing this for him?

Maybe partly—and his reaction? So worth it.

'Merle?' he asked again. 'Why are you chuckling to yourself?'

'I'm thinking that I don't care what anyone thinks.' She smiled, aware of her blossoming sensuality and confidence. 'Except you. But I know you like my outfit.'

'Not just your outfit.'

A ripple of sensual awareness skimmed down her spine. The pleasure, the sensations, of this evening? Stepping out with him, teasing him, enjoying every mouthful of that stunning food, the restaurant's stylish decor and the sexy beats from the live band by the dance floor... *Everything* had been perfect. It wasn't an experience she wanted to just remember, but an experience that she wanted *again*.

Ash Castle had opened up her world. He'd pulled her free of the shroud beneath which she'd hidden for so long—*not* her coverall, but her tendency to stay safe back in the shadows. He'd given her more than he'd promised. More than the sexuality she felt safe exploring with him, more than the light jokes and games between them. More than the serious conversation too.

But there was another, rarer element curling around all these things, threading them together, forming an unbreakable, undeniable core within her. Something invisible, something strong, had melded to her central framework and become inseparable from her very soul. She gazed up at him, lost in the world of memory and sensation, laughter, spark and sensuality. The world that was totally, utterly Ash.

* * *

Ash's clothes felt too tight. His collar especially. It made breathing difficult. Thinking was simply impossible. That weird protectiveness rearing within tensed all of his muscles. But Merle held him close. She had rhythm. But then, he knew that, didn't he? She moved so well in his arms. In sync and breathing together, they sensed and anticipated each other's movements.

He was desperate to be alone with her. Yet he didn't want to short-change her on the night out he'd promised. But she cupped his jaw. And she tempted him.

'Shall we continue this dance upstairs?' she murmured.

She saved him.

As the lift rose, taking them to their hotel suite, his tension scorched. 'Merle…'

'Yes?'

Something broke apart within him then. Her simple, sweet response. Affirmative. Listening. Willing.

It was everything he wanted from her. And it terrified him at the same time. He had no idea how he unlocked the hotel room or what he did with the damn key card, just that somehow they were inside the door and alone. Thank heavens.

This wasn't just superficial desire, but also physical need underpinned by bone-deep longing. A fast release wasn't going to work. But he was unable to stop himself from trying. The sexiest outfit ever had just become the source of the most insane frustration. Somehow he worked it out and the scarlet shimmered down her body in a slither of sexy colour and then she stood so close to naked, clad only in a tiny bra and thong, in matching scarlet. Ash had never felt as honoured in his life. Not even their first night together compared to this. He was utterly lost for words.

She smiled at him again. 'Thank you for tonight. It was a lot of fun.'

Fun? He couldn't stand the compressed sensation inside his chest. It was as if his heart had been clamped by some medieval instrument of torture. He couldn't bear to look into her beautiful eyes but he couldn't look away and something once held fast slipped loose inside. In another breath, every last semblance of his control was lost.

He tore the condom wrapper between his teeth. Her eyes widened with humour and arousal. A gorgeous, intoxicating, provocative mix that made him even more desperate to take her. Now. To his eternal gratitude she stepped forward and reached for his belt, intuitively understanding the level of pain he was in right now. Two strokes of her gentle hand up his turgid length was two too many for him to handle. He growled. Her gaze lifted to his. A smoky, sensual pride gleamed in those brown eyes.

He buried his thoughts by kissing her, rejoicing because it wasn't a response that she gave him, it was an action of her own—the dance of her tongue against his, the slide she'd learned so quickly, tore at the last of his self-restraint. The way she wanted him destroyed him. This was a pure celebration of their physical selves— of desire and pleasure to be found with each other. But it wasn't just that. The sudden tightness in his chest hurt.

He spun her to face the wall so he couldn't see her expressive face, because he was so close to something else. He hooked his thumbs into the waistband of that tiny scarlet thong and tugged it down. Seconds later he'd unhooked her bra and taken a moment to skim his palms across her tight-budded breasts before sliding his hands to settle heavy and hard on her hips, holding her where he needed her to be. This was sex. This was just another night. This meant *nothing* more. But then she braced her hands on the wall in front of her and pushed back, sliding her curvy derriere into him. Claiming her space. No longer hiding, no longer content to be invisible— not around him.

He could only take pleasure in her stance. Pressing her against the wall. And she was hot and wet, the silken pull of her muscles sending his into overdrive. He tensed at the base of his spine. His release so close. Too close. Too soon.

He fought to regain himself and slow it down. But her hair was loose and fragrant and her moans of delight, of demand, rang in his ears. He couldn't resist pressing a kiss at the side of her neck and once there he was lost, tempted again by those sweet, small earlobes just made for him to nibble. She shuddered and cried out, her lithe body shaking. Passion and pleasure rushed over him at her response. His skin rippled as goose pimples lifted everywhere. He swiftly slipped his hand down to delve and delight her and heard her harsh, high-pitched cry of pleasure. He closed his eyes but the shock waves of her detonation went through him anyway and sucked the last of his control with it. He gripped her tightly and pumped hard, all control gone.

His heart slammed against his ribs. He didn't want

it to be over. He didn't want this just to be…that. A night. A good time. A meaningless moment. Because that was the last thing this was for him. This felt like so much more and, even though he'd tried to deny it, he couldn't any more. He tried again—slammed on the mental brakes, trying to stem the unfettered feelings flooding his body.

He wasn't even undressed. His trousers were around his ankles as though he were some out-of-control teen. His shirt was stuck to his back, slick with sweat from the searing heat she'd roused in him. He'd ravished her. He could feel her legs trembling as she rested her forehead against her arms, taking support from the wall in front of her.

'I'm sorry,' he groaned. 'Too fast.'

But she tilted her head back, resting against his shoulder and exposing the long, vulnerable column of her throat, and laughed. A brief, sexy chuckle that rang with pleasure and unvarnished, unashamed *pride*.

The jumble of concern in his head faded away. 'You liked that?'

She chuckled again. 'You seemed as if…'

'As if?' he said quietly. 'As if I couldn't stop myself? As if I couldn't wait? As if I wanted nothing more than to be locked in here with you? Because that's exactly what happened.'

At the dewy, deliciously dirty satisfaction in her eyes he was hard again. And, given the way she pressed her lithe, lissom body back against his, she knew exactly what she'd just done. She was the sweetest vixen. He'd forgotten that this was supposed to only be sex.

He'd forgotten that it was ending. He'd forgotten that he couldn't give her what she most needed.

All he wanted now was to make love to her for hours and hours.

CHAPTER TEN

MERLE SIPPED HER fresh-squeezed orange juice and wondered whether she should wake him. For the third time in the hour she opted not to. He needed the rest. And she needed more time to *process*. Last night had been... *indescribable*. No words could explain the sensations she was still floating upon. The intensity followed by such tenderness. He'd kissed her, kissed her, kissed her. Now she tried to stay in the present, tried not to panic about the fact the week was almost over and he'd be returning to Australia soon. She had to be grateful for the experience, right?

But she wanted more.

She wanted the man who'd come apart before her very eyes last night. She wanted more of that kick to the heart she'd felt when she'd seen his reaction to her scarlet jumpsuit. That thrill of pleasure. She wanted more of his attention, his wit, his warmth.

'Merle? Why didn't you wake me?' He walked through the door already dressed in those dark denim jeans and tee that skimmed his muscular frame.

He looked as if he'd had a hard night—his hair rumpled, stubble on his jaw, the sight of which sent a tingle to her fingertips. She wanted to touch him all over again. She didn't want the night to be over. Ever.

'You were in a really deep sleep,' she said huskily.

For a moment their gazes meshed. But his lips twisted and his lashes lowered. 'Come on. We'd better get back. I've missed a bunch of messages from the pilot.'

'Oh—'

'It doesn't matter,' he said negligently. 'He'll be ready the minute we get there.'

She nodded. Things moved that way for Ash. Instantly and at his summons. Because he didn't want to stay.

Her heart sank as she realised. He *never* stayed.

Ash strode across the tarmac, gritting his teeth to suppress another yawn. Strange, he'd never felt this exhausted. Maybe he was coming down with the flu? Maybe that would explain his behaviour last night. He'd never lost control like that. Never been so overcome by lust he'd barely paused long enough to ensure his partner was there with him. But Merle had been. In fact, she'd been a step ahead. He'd heard it in her breathing, seen it in her glazed eyes, felt it in every inch of her body. She'd stayed a step ahead of him the rest of the night too. She was still a step ahead of him now. He followed her into the helicopter. He didn't speak. The bright sunlight made his eyes ache.

Last Friday he'd arrived on Waiheke at night and the house had been cloaked in dusky darkness. For the first day he'd focused on the pool. Then he'd been so focused on Merle he'd not noticed the property—he'd avoided it. But this time, the midday sun was bright and he was so focused on *not* looking at Merle that he couldn't help but see it. *All* of it. A wall of hurt and regret slammed into him. The helicopter lifted up as soon as they were clear and walking towards that wretched lawn court. In only a few minutes silence returned. He glanced to see Merle watching him. Beyond her, the house loomed. He couldn't decide which caused him the most discomfort.

'This is the last time I'll be here,' he muttered unthinkingly. He had to be done with it.

'This week.' She nodded.

'At all,' he corrected flatly.

She paused on the path. 'You're not coming back?' Her soft lips parted on an audible breath. 'Are you planning to sell it?'

Her shock lifted his heart for a second—before it smashed back down like a stone hitting concrete.

'Why does that surprise you?' he asked. Surely she understood this place held little happiness for him?

'You love it here.'

'No.' His blood ran cold here. 'I wasn't going to come back at all. But in the end I couldn't let it go without...'

He growled, because he'd never expressed it aloud—never wanted to. But he was tired and somehow he couldn't resist the compulsion to tell *her*. As if she were justice herself—a scale with which he could weigh the decision—even though he already knew it tipped him towards guilty.

'I had to see what he'd done to wreck the place,' he muttered in frustration.

'You think this is *wrecked*?' Merle's gaze shot back to the house briefly before returning to shine that steadfast belief into his. 'Ash, this place is beautiful—'

'You're wrong. It *was* beautiful.'

She didn't understand the level—or the layers—of destruction. She didn't know that the last time he'd visited was branded in his brain and had left a wound that would never heal. He'd regret the pain he'd caused for the rest of his life. There could be no redemption. His mistakes were unforgivable.

'The heart of it got ripped out, and a new facade put in place,' he said gruffly. 'It looks like perfection but there's nothing real.'

His skin tightened but the misery swelling within couldn't be contained. He stood even more rigidly, re-sisting the threatening emotional explosion. He didn't want this. He couldn't even walk inside. Instead he gazed around the garden.

'Ash?'

'There used to be an orchard where the tennis court is,' he muttered. 'Apples, peaches, plums... I used to climb up and pick something and take it to where Mum was watching from the balcony. She always knew where the best ones were but she let me find them.'

He was too lost in memory to register the long pause.

'That would've been awesome,' Merle eventually responded with her softness.

'They ripped it out when they put in the bunker and the tennis court.' He stared at the green expanse that had shocked him so completely. 'The garden was every-thing to her. She couldn't do the physical work but she designed it. She was good friends with the grounds-man and they kept a record of the produce each year.' He surveyed it, remembering how much there'd once been. 'I guess nothing of any real depth can grow when there's a lump of cold metal just beneath the surface.'

Which was him too, right? Fine superficially, but beneath—what was there really? For the first time he felt how lacking in depth, how empty inside he was. A sense of futility stunned him—for all of his success, his years proving to his father that he didn't need him, that he could do better than him. What, exactly, had it all been for? His father had foisted the inheritance on him anyway. Ignoring Ash's years of anger and absence. He'd still assumed that Ash was his true son—*just like him*, the worthy recipient of what he'd created.

'I haven't been back here in almost a decade,' he admitted quietly.

Friday night had been the first time he'd seen that the trees had been replaced with perfect lawn, that the comfortable old house had been renovated into soullessness with stripped-back decor and nothing intimate or personal about the place. He knew it was maintained by a team of strangers who swooped in and set everything 'just so'. Even now, a year after his father's death, they maintained its flawless facade. It irritated him intensely. Even after his death his father was all about false appearances. About destroying what should have been wonderful—purely because of *greed*. Everything had been an investment, but Hugh didn't value true treasure. Like those damned trees.

'Why haven't you been in so long?'

He'd simply been unable to. But it had come to a point when he couldn't avoid it any longer.

'After Mum died, I fell out with my father. I refused to have anything to do with him or the company,

I avoided all our properties and built my own,' he said.
'Now I've finally come back and discovered my worst
nightmare was reality. He's scrubbed everything of her
from the place. He's destroyed everything she'd created
to fulfil some stupid desire for some gadget he thought
was essential.'

'You came here a lot before she died?'

'When Mum's health declined, she moved here permanently.'

Merle stood very still beside him. 'But your dad was
still in Sydney?'

He nodded. He could hear the confusion in her voice.
He'd already told her his family life had been more of a
family lie. But she still didn't realise just how messed
up it had been. And he couldn't seem to stop himself
from remembering.

'Did you divide your time between them?' Merle
asked when he didn't immediately answer.

'I went to a very *prestigious* boarding school a few
hours north of Sydney,' he explained with full sarcasm.
'It offered every advantage for a young person, you
know. Then I'd come here for the holidays.'

He had rarely seen his father—so he didn't impact
on the secret lifestyle his father had enjoyed. Glancing
over, he saw her deepening frown, and Ash shook his
head. 'Yeah, no denying my teenage years were dys-
functional.'

'But why do you want to sell it now?' she asked. 'I
don't think you hate this place, Ash. I think you still
love it. It's just that you were hurt here. Maybe being
here makes you remember what you lost.'

Being here made him angry. And powerless. Because there was no fixing any of it.

'Mum's passing was awful,' he admitted. In an almost naive way he hadn't realised how ill she was. He'd thought she would go on as she was for years—in a kind of weak but strong stasis. He'd thought he'd have a chance to make things right again once she'd got over her anger. But there'd been no chance. 'I'd already lost everything before that. Because *I'm* the one who inflicted the pain here.'

Her steady, unflinching gaze stabilised his careering emotions.

'What happened?'

He'd known she'd ask. Who wouldn't when given a statement like that? He'd wanted her to. He wanted her to know. Because then? Then she'd know the truth. She'd know him for who he was. And that light in her eyes when she looked at him? That would dim.

'It was my fault my mother died when she did,' he said harshly.

'What?' Merle's soft voice lifted. 'How?'

'I broke her heart.' And it had already been so damaged, the harm was irreparable. His own heart tore every time he so much as thought of it.

But Merle stayed still, her gaze true and calm. 'How did you do that?'

'I proved to her that I was just like him.'

Didn't I teach you to play fair? Not to cheat? Never cheat, Ashton.

His mother's recriminations echoed. Even after all this time they scalded his vital organs, making it feel impossible to breathe. If he told Merle the whole truth she'd recoil. She'd step back. She was too much of a believer in good things not to shrink away from something awful. And maybe after last night that would be best. Because last night had changed this.

'I cheated,' he added bluntly. 'Just like him.'

And the fallout had sent him on a spiralling path of excess and oblivion—pointedly different to his dad's secrecy. Ash had been boldly, openly provocative. He'd developed his own code.

But Merle didn't flinch. She merely nodded, almost matter-of-factly. 'That girl—when you were young.'

It hadn't been a matter-of-fact mistake. 'Her name was Rose Gold.'

At a muffled sound from Merle he grinned ruefully. 'Yeah. Trust me, no one hates that more than she does.'

'But you were at school.'

'She came to my boarding school, yes.'

'So this was a youthful, schoolboy mistake. Secondary school,' she reiterated.

But it had been no minor indiscretion and the awful repercussions had been permanent. Merle still gazed up at him, clearly waiting, and, as much as he regretted starting this, the anger within made him continue. She needed to know what he'd done.

'It wasn't teenage foolishness, it was massive. Rose was in the year below mine but she was even younger. One of those super-smart kids, she'd been accelerated up. Apparently we'd already met because she was the daughter of one of my mother's friends, but honestly I didn't remember her. Mum asked me to be kind, ensure she was included. She was shy. I think she'd been unwell or something.' He sighed. 'She was pretty nerdy.

A society princess but shy at that point.' He paused and frowned as he realised Merle's skin had pinkened.

'Come on,' he muttered. 'We should get out of the sun. It's burning at this time of day.'

But Merle resisted. 'Tell me what happened.'

'I will, when you're in the shade.'

Merle walked ahead of him again but once she'd passed the pool she turned and blocked his way into the house.

'Okay, I'm in the shade. Tell me the rest.'

Ash grimaced. 'I became her champion, I guess. I didn't think anything of it. People assumed we were dating because I'd sought her out and she hadn't said anything to the contrary. It amused me to see her popularity rise. I didn't take it too seriously. I didn't think she had either. We weren't exactly physical—I thought we were more friends. But she was flattered, I guess.'

'I bet she…' Merle mumbled. 'I bet she had a massive crush on you.'

'I only asked her to go to that damn dance because Mum asked me to. To make sure she had a good time. But I…'

'What happened at the dance?'

He shifted on his feet, obviously uncomfortable. 'I got filmed with another girl.'

'Filmed? Oh…' Merle's gaze slid from his.

'Two girls, actually,' he confessed angrily. 'I got stood down from school for misconduct. Never went back. Got summoned here. Mum was more furious than I'd ever seen her. *How could I have done that to Rose?* She tore strips off me. *"You're just like him."* Direct quote.'

'Ash—'

'The thing was, I'd not known. About Dad, I mean. I didn't know *any* of it until that afternoon. I'd never seen Mum so agitated. She cried about things that didn't make sense. Later, I asked her what she'd meant but she'd calmed down and shut me out and wouldn't say. She sent me away. Back to Sydney. To Dad. And I found out the truth.'

The lies. The cheating. The absolute betrayal.

'Do you know what he did?' He looked at Merle.

Merle tried to stay calm, but every muscle had tensed. She was still reconciling what he'd told her about that girl, Rose. A shy, quiet girl whom he'd humiliated so *publicly*. But this about his father was going to be bad too. No son had such a visceral reaction to the mere mention of his father without serious reason.

'Leo Castle isn't my only half-sibling,' Ash said harshly. 'It wasn't just that Dad was a serial cheater and lazy when it came to contraception. He was a risk-taker who didn't think he'd ever get caught.' He flinched at his inward recollections. 'It turned out he'd also seduced my aunt. Mum's younger sister. So my cousin Grace is actually my half-sister. That's why she was so angry with me for turning out just like him, *despite* her efforts.'

'But you're not like him.'

'No? Not selfish? Not arrogant? Not a cheater?' He shook his head. 'I never saw Mum again,' he muttered. 'She died less than a week after she'd sent me back in disgrace.'

The deeply etched pain in his voice scraped Merle's nerves.

'I literally broke her heart.'

Merle ached for the horror and guilt he felt. 'I think your father might've already done that, Ash.'

His eyes widened and for a moment he froze. 'But I ripped it right through,' he said hoarsely. 'I was the one thing she believed in. I let her down. And she died.'

'Ash—'

'I'd had no idea he was unfaithful at all, let alone so completely,' he said hurriedly. 'It's embarrassing when with adult hindsight it's so bloody obvious. I had to find out what she'd meant. I confronted him when I got there. He didn't even try to deny it. He was more interested in the details of what had happened with those girls in the bathroom at the dance. He actually *congratulated* me. He said I needed to work on my discretion, but he was proud. That's when I realised what he was like. I searched online and found a reference to Leo in an old newspaper. I tracked him down and offered to do the DNA test for him to prove our dad's paternity.' Ash's smile was both satisfied and sad. 'My father never forgave me for *that*. He was so angry, he admitted the truth about Grace with vindictive pleasure. He said I couldn't escape who I was—his son. With his flaws. His predilections. And he was right. I'd already proved that. So I acted out, with no discretion at all.'

'It was *one* mistake, Ash.'

He shook his head. 'I was careless and selfish and went for what I wanted then and there.'

'But you learned from it. You said you've never cheated since.'

'I've never had a relationship since.'

'To be honest, it doesn't sound like it was much of a relationship with Rose.'

He paused. 'No. We never even slept together but it meant more to her. I think I knew that and I didn't want it and I took the coward's way out to end it. I broke her trust and I humiliated her.'

Merle felt a horrible affinity for the girl. She could understand how easy it would be to fall—to imagine there might be more—when Ash Castle had his full attention on you. 'Where's Rose now?'

'Still at university, I think. An academic. Very good at…her subject.'

Merle smiled a little sadly, feeling for Rose. 'You don't know what it is, do you?'

'She's not spoken to me since and I don't blame her.' He winced. 'People had phones everywhere… I just didn't want…'

'To say it to her face?' she guessed.

'It was like I'd kicked a kitten.' He rubbed his face.

Merle could imagine all too well how mortified poor Rose must have been. Then Ash had been sent away from the school. It would've been horrendous to have been left there with everyone in her class knowing. And she would have had such a crush. It was impossible not to crush on Ash Castle.

But, while he'd made a mistake, Ash's *world* had been obliterated. He'd disappointed the one person who mattered to him most. He'd discovered appalling, devastating truths. He'd have felt such shame for his father. And in turn himself.

'You didn't get to see your mother again?' she asked softly.

He stood very still, not looking at her, not seeming to see anything but the bitter memories lodged inside. 'We didn't even speak on the phone. I was angry because I felt guilty. Angry because I was shocked. *Everything* had been a lie. Her husband had an affair with her own sister. Can you imagine the betrayal?' He closed his eyes briefly. 'And it happened when they both knew she was unwell. That was why I'm the only child. The only one she could have and I...' He pushed out a heavy sigh. 'Hell, no wonder Grace never holidayed with us here.' He glared at the pool and then turned that tortured gaze back on Merle. 'Why didn't she leave him? Why did she stay and put up with that for so long?'

She understood why he asked. Ash hadn't stayed. He'd been so hurt, felt such guilt, he'd rejected his father totally. But his anguish and the questioning of his mother's hard choices were ultimately unanswerable. Merle could only guess, only imagine.

'Maybe she didn't have the strength,' she suggested gently. 'Maybe the battle for her health was the only one she had the energy to fight.'

He didn't reply for a long time.

'What was she like?' Merle asked.

'When she had the energy, she was so much fun.' His expression fell again. 'And I devastated her. I broke her heart.'

'But you *didn't* kill her, Ash,' Merle said softly. 'She'd been unwell a long time, right?'

His nod was jerky.

'And you weren't much more than a kid yourself.

Packed off to boarding school. Isolated from your parents through a very sad time. Burdened with a ton of external expectation and no real support to help you cope. I'm not surprised you sought a way out—however you could—especially at that age, when everything's overwhelming. You were so alone.'

'Don't feel sorry for me, Merle. I don't deserve it.'

She disagreed. He was beating himself up over something that had happened a long time ago. A series of events had morphed together into a tangle from which he'd drawn conclusions that weren't necessarily true. She could understand how he had when such deep, devastated emotions were at play. That was because of the person Ash was. And *that* was the point.

'You're different from your father,' she said urgently, aching for him to believe her. But she saw his instant negation. 'You are—'

'Some things can't be changed,' he interrupted bitterly. 'I am who I am.'

'Workaholic, fiery, full of energy and independence,' she said. 'And you try to hide it, but you're a man who *cares*.'

He turned a burning gaze on her but she held it defiantly, daring him to deny it.

'I don't believe you want to give this place up, Ash.'

'I can't keep it like this.' He glanced across at the lawn again. 'He destroyed everything she built.'

'Then rebuild it. No one says you can't do what you want with it. Things can change, Ash. People can too.'

'Eternally optimistic, aren't you?' But his small smile didn't reach his eyes.

'I don't see that as a negative.' She put her hand on

his arm, hoping to somehow get him to believe her. 'Everyone makes mistakes. Everyone screws up. Everyone hurts someone—intentionally or not. That's part of being human,' she said. 'Maybe the trick isn't to try to erase it, or even to ease it, but just to accept that it happened. That it's there. So there's a little weight you carry and maybe you'll always have it, but that's okay.' Beneath her hand, she felt his tension. 'Because you'd do things differently now, right?' she said softly. 'Facing the same situation now, you wouldn't do that again.'

'Of course not.'

'So—' she smiled '—you've learned something. It's just very sad you didn't get to see your mother again so she could see that too. And it's sad your father took everything of hers away. I'm so sorry he did that.'

Ash looked directly at her again. She saw pain in his amber eyes. And tiredness.

'Thanks, Merle.' A gruff whisper of appreciation.

Yet Merle felt as if he was slipping away from her. That her words hadn't comforted him at all—they'd been futile. Like seeds scattered on hardened, dry land.

He stepped away. 'I think I need a swim.'

She watched him walk away, feeling oddly bereft. This morning she'd dressed in the scarlet jumpsuit she'd worn last night. Partly because the silk felt heavenly against her sensitive skin but mostly because she hadn't wanted her fairy-tale night to be over yet. But the heat of the day had built and now the sunlight was harsh. He'd been right. It had been seconds away from burning her skin. And what he'd told her lingered. The parallels she felt with Rose made her wince. How easy it would've been to wish there might be more meaning in

Ash's actions. He'd have been spellbinding, a force of nature even then, with that ferocity of intent. But she also knew how easy it was to misinterpret someone's intentions. And *he'd* certainly learned from the resultant horror. He didn't let any woman get the wrong impression now. Not relationships. Only sex. And in business he'd been driven to succeed on a scale impossible to most people, desperate to build something bigger and better than his father.

Her heart ached for him as she showered and dressed. He was still swimming length after length, so she didn't interrupt him. She sensed he needed time to clear his head. So she went in search of a displacement activity of her own.

It was another two hours till he came in. He was back in his shorts, a white tee skimming his broad chest. Her heart bumped against her ribcage.

'What have you been up to?' He didn't quite meet her gaze.

She didn't want things to be awkward, so she tried to keep it light as she surveyed the mess she'd made in the kitchen. 'I cooked dinner. Elevated instant noodles.'

He shot her a glance. To her relief the old smile flickered in his eyes. 'Elevated? They're still instant noodles.'

'Are you not prepared to give them a chance?' she asked primly.

'I'll try them. For you.'

The merest hint of his old flirt lifted a bubble of hope in her. She set dinner out on the table of one of the smaller dining nooks, still with a stunning view across the bay, and opened another bottle of champagne.

'Champagne with noodles?' he queried.

'The perfect accompaniment.'

'And is that lobster tail I see in there?' He stirred the contents of his steaming bowl with a fork and began to laugh.

'Elevated, as I said.' She grinned impishly at him. 'Isn't it amazing how satisfying something can be, even when it's pulled together from sparse ingredients?'

He shot her a look across the table. 'I don't think we can consider lobster sparse.'

'Still full of flavour and delicious. Still satisfying.' She wilfully ignored his interruption. 'And yet it can still leave you wanting more.'

His lips twitched and she finally saw him fully relax with a long sigh. 'Oh, Merle. I definitely want more.'

CHAPTER ELEVEN

MERLE WALKED THROUGH the eerily quiet house. It was stupid but she was almost afraid to call out to him—afraid there would be no reply. So she crept quietly, slowly searching each space, hoping to find him. Fearing she wouldn't. While 'playful' Ash had reappeared last night at dinner, by the time they'd gone to bed he'd fallen silent. But he hadn't slept. He'd turned to her—touched her, taken her with a wordless, gentle intimacy that had been different yet again. The tender intensity had devastated her, yet she'd held him too—feeling the emotions humming within him. It hadn't been a fiercely passionate escape into the physical. It had been deeper than that—there'd been no escape from the emotion, there'd been a silent exposition of it. Of need. Of wonder. Of connectedness. And she'd loved it. Loved *him*. Until she'd finally fallen asleep, still holding him close.

But when she'd woken only five minutes ago, he was already gone. She'd touched his pillow, and there was no residual warmth. No sleeping in for a second time for Ash.

She glanced out from the balcony but the water in the pool was still. The bay in the distance was a pure landscape, no human or other animal giving movement to the picture-perfect landscape. She walked through to the kitchen but it was empty. It felt like the whole place was oddly untouched. A horrible premonition ate away her security. Had he left already? Without even saying goodbye?

Anxiety shot nausea to the back of her throat. Because she knew now—this wasn't some light affair for her. Not some fun 'experience' that she might go on to have again with some other guy. There'd never be another guy. Not like Ash. What she felt for him? It was immense and overwhelming and so wonderful that it terrified her.

But he didn't want it, did he? She fervently, desperately wished he did or would. She needed more time with him. They needed so much more time. So where was he now?

She checked the pool again. The study. For a moment she wondered about the bunker, but then she heard a sound in the distance. Walking around the side of the house, she saw one of the garage doors open.

'Ash?' She blinked, her eyes adjusting to the change from the bright morning sunlight to the dim interior. There were towers of boxes she'd yet to open and categorise. But Ash had ripped open several and was standing in the centre of a pile of stuff.

'What are you doing?' she asked.

He glanced up at her grimly. The emotion that he usually kept so deeply buried was now glinting sharply in his eyes. This place dredged it up. Increasingly over this last week memories had risen until he'd been so bothered, he'd been devastatingly honest with her. He'd revealed that wellspring of pain—the mistake he'd made that had unleashed the truth of his parents' marriage and what he feared had hastened his mother's death. Merle had hoped that, just by listening, she might've helped. But now? She didn't think she had. A trouble shared wasn't always a trouble halved. It was still just a trouble.

'I'm sorry for making a mess and making your job worse than it already was,' he said gruffly.

She didn't care about the mess. She cared about him. But he was avoiding looking at her again.

'Were you searching for something in particular?' she asked.

He stood stiffly in the centre of that heap. Merle saw some of the paperwork was damaged. Water must've somehow gotten into those boxes.

'I thought, maybe, in all the boxes, there might've been something worth keeping. You know, didn't he want to keep my old swimming trophies?' The bitterest smile barely curved his lips as he shrugged sarcastically. 'I guess not. It's all just his stuff. He expunged every *last* thing of us both. There's nothing of her. None of her diaries. The garden journals.'

He'd wanted something of his mother's to treasure. And he'd not found it. His desolation swept over her.

'I guess he only kept her games because they were in good condition and valuable,' he said. 'Not because he wanted any real reminder of her. They're an investment. Like everything he held on to.'

Had he once considered Ash an investment too? The heir groomed to take over the company? The one he was proud to have follow in his footsteps? Whom he'd wanted to corrupt? And the man had shipped his wife to a whole other country. Out of sight and out of mind for her final years. Merle hated him.

'Why do you think he kept that one photo?' she asked.

'For show. He probably put it face down when he was here. Or,' he added acidly, 'maybe he used it as a reminder to his new lovers that he'd already had a wife and child and didn't plan on making that same mistake again.'

'Ash—'

'It's true. Apparently he vowed he'd never marry again after Mum died. But it wasn't because he was heartbroken. He just didn't want the expense of a divorce. He collected girlfriends—a new model every couple of years in the decade before he died. There would've been more, of course, those ones on the side he had in secret. So he could still look like the loyal, grieving widower.' Still not meeting her gaze, he kicked at the pile at his feet. 'I can't believe you have to go through all of this.'

'It's my job to go through everything. It's not personal for me the way it is for you. It's not painful.'

His jaw clamped.

'Why don't you come inside and have breakfast?' she suggested.

'Food isn't going to make this better, Merle. I'm not a hangry two-year-old.'

Ash couldn't stand to see the disbelief he knew ought to instantly flash on Merle's face. He couldn't even manage a joke. The irritation scratching down his spinal cord like nails on a chalkboard was impossible to ignore. And his irascibility, his impatience, was all amplified *because* he was so irritated and he knew he shouldn't be. He shouldn't care at all. He'd thought he hadn't for so long.

He was supposed to have come here briefly to see what had been done to it and to sever all ties. An acidic, isolated homage to all that had been and all that he couldn't change. He should've been able to handle that. Then he'd discovered *she* was staying here. Merle. His own house nymph—all temptation and temporary effervescence. He should've been able to handle her too. Except she'd put *possibilities* into his head. And he'd stayed. He'd taken what he shouldn't. He'd done so many things that he never allowed himself to do.

Now he couldn't even hold eye contact with her.

He stared down at the piles he'd rummaged through in a furious frenzy this morning. They were now scattered in a haphazard mess at his feet. Any remnant 'piles' had tumbled into a shambolic heap. He didn't know why he'd thought he'd actually find anything that mattered.

'No wonder you like to wear the gloves and the hazmat suit,' he growled.

'The boxes shouldn't have been put straight onto the floor,' she said. 'I'll fix that. Dry out these items and prevent more damage.'

Her tone was soft and gentle. As if *he* was the object being treated with kid gloves. That irritated him even more. He didn't deserve gentleness. He didn't want her or anyone touching this rubbish. It really all ought to be put on a bonfire. But he didn't mention it. He couldn't seem to manage a joke. 'I'll put it back in the boxes for now.'

'Do you want some help?'

He certainly couldn't look into her eyes now. He knew he'd see sympathy and concern. And other things.

'No.' He didn't want anything from her.

'Ash—'

'You should go and have breakfast,' he dismissed her abruptly. 'I'll be along in a bit.'

There was the barest hesitation before she left.

Ash drew in a sharp breath because now he knew. Last night something ordinarily impossible had briefly become imaginable—like a wisp of a magical fog that promised growth. But that wisp had evaporated in this morning's light. All that remained here now was a musty, mildewy pile of meaningless *stuff*. There was nothing worth keeping. Especially not now the rot had set in.

He needed to leave.

He'd thought this trip would be simple enough. That he wouldn't care. Instead, he'd discovered he still loved the place. Even with the changes there was something that would always move him here. And, in showing it to Merle, he'd remembered moments beyond those last painful ones when he'd faced his mother's disappointment. Ironically, the hurt that came with those other memories was almost worse.

He'd tried to bury himself in Merle to avoid it all again. Only he'd woken this morning with the realisation that *she* was the problem too. Not just part of it but as much of a *cause* as any old memory. She'd shown him the world through her eyes, with an appreciation that was somehow contagious. She'd shown him *more* than this place: she'd shown him herself. And what had he done? He'd told her everything. Because she was real and right here. And she'd been gentle and accepting and she'd wrapped him in that wispy mirage of something impossible. He'd believed in it. In what she'd said. The importance of small things. So he'd come to check this morning. But it hadn't taken long for reality to return. There was no point in unsealing old boxes. Not when the contents were half-rotten and couldn't be fixed. Not when there was so little of any value left.

And when the wisps of promise were blown away, the truth remained. That hesitation he'd felt when she'd first come to him? He should have rejected her offer that night. Because the gorgeous Merle was asking for something in her bottomless eyes that he could never, ever give her. She deserved so much more. Even if he tried, he knew that in the end he couldn't deliver. It wasn't in his DNA to be there for someone, or to promise not to let them down. He could never guarantee that he wouldn't disappoint her. He couldn't bear to do that.

So he needed to leave here. He needed to leave *her*. And he needed to leave *now*.

Merle didn't know what had changed in Ash's thinking, or why. All she knew was that he was restless and angry. The usual amusement—even sarcastic joking—had been snuffed from his eyes. Her tension built the longer he stayed away.

Anxiety made her want to hide. To slip back to the shadows and stay safe. But she fought it. She wouldn't retreat into those old habits.

He didn't join her for breakfast, so she ate alone. She went for a quick swim, splashing a little extra-loudly, but he didn't appear. He didn't invite her for a ride on the boat or challenge her to a game. Two hours passed excruciatingly slowly. In the end, she decided to catalogue some effects in the study because she didn't know what else to do. The loss of time pressed like a sharp blade against the sensitive, thin skin of her neck—the sense of danger, of desperation tightened. Tomorrow would be Sunday—a full week since their bargain. Which meant he was due to leave. So this was their last day together. Shouldn't it be good—couldn't they forget that ticking clock for just a little longer?

Despite the warmth of the sun beating onto the deck, she felt chilled to the bone. Seconds staggered by slower than a sloth crossing a stretch of forest floor. Something was wrong. He'd gone from being open—being vulnerable—to being both physically and emotionally remote. It devastated her. Because last night they'd made love. She'd known the difference. There'd been an unspoken but deep empathy—that caring, that tenderness in their touch. She'd embraced him, showing her understanding, wanting him to know she understood, that she was here for him. Accepted him as he was. It hadn't just been fun, hadn't just been pleasurable. He'd *held* her and she'd held him back. Hadn't that meant something?

Was it his departure that was bothering him now? Was he too wondering whether this situation—this time between them—could be extended? Maybe he might even consider coming back for another visit while she was still working here?

No. It wasn't important enough for him to even

think about. He was working through the agony of his history here.

'Merle?'

That bubble of hope rose from her belly into the tightness in her chest—pushing for breathing space.

'I'm in the study,' she called.

But she followed the direction of his voice and stepped out through one of the glass doors, onto the deck by the pool. The second she saw him that bubble got stuck—instant ice stopping its upward float. Ash was dressed, actually *dressed,* in dark denim jeans and a creaseless grey tee that hugged his hewn body. But it was the shoes that gripped her attention. They were not casual trainers or poolside sandals, but boots. Shoes for a journey.

'Are you going somewhere?' She hoped he'd deny what was so obvious.

'I need to get back to Sydney.'

That bubble inside her burst. 'To do what?'

He didn't reply. He was regarding her so seriously, but she could read the thoughts in his eyes. There was nothing urgent for him to go back to.

'I have meetings to prepare for,' he muttered.

'You can't do that here?'

She didn't know why she maintained the fiction with him. Why she didn't just challenge him outright to speak the truth.

In answer he simply shook his head.

'Why not?' she asked.

'The environment is too distracting.' A wisp of a smile.

But Merle couldn't smile. That he was leaving was

bad enough. That this was over was devastating. But that he was ending it *earlier* than she'd expected? Right when the balance had tipped and it had become raw, but so good? Right when they were on the brink of something so much more? He was stealing away all possibility. Denying them any kind of chance—this was like someone tipping over the board and scattering the pieces before the game was won.

It *hurt*.

Because it meant he didn't care. His time with her had been good, but not good enough. *Distracting* but not anything important enough or meaningful enough to stick around or change plans for. Except he *had* changed plans. Hadn't he shortened it? Her gaze narrowed as she tried to understand *why* he was ending this *sooner*. If she was just a distraction, if this wasn't that meaningful, why, then, did he have to escape here—and her—earlier? That bubble reformed and floated up again.

'You've had enough time here?' she asked.

He didn't move.

'Enough of me?' she asked. 'You don't want one more night?'

He swallowed but still didn't answer.

'Are you running away, Ash?'

His jaw clenched. 'It was always coming to an end, Merle. That was the agreement.'

'Agreement?' As if this really was some sort of bloodless business arrangement? As if emotions hadn't tangled between them? 'Why now, though? You've ended the game early. Reneged. Why?'

'You're that determined to have your last night with me?'

She paused, then stepped forward, which took all her

courage. 'Why does it have to be the last night at all?' she asked bravely. 'You could come back here while I'm still working.'

He didn't give an inch. 'I told you I'm never coming back.'

'Aren't you allowed to change your mind?' she asked. 'You told me I could change my mind any time. Why are the rules different for you?'

His expression hardened. 'You know I don't go past one night. Our fling was only longer because of… circumstance. I thought you understood that.'

It wasn't because of circumstance. He'd *chosen*. And so had she. 'You don't think things have changed?'

He didn't waver. 'No.'

'You don't think this matters more than some brief fling?' Her voice wobbled. '*I* don't matter more?'

'Merle—'

'Don't lie,' she interrupted. 'Don't offer a platitude. Be honest. Why are you leaving early?'

'Because I can't stand to stay here a second longer.'

The buzzing sound in her ears was getting louder. It wasn't an internal hum of frustration, it was a real noise. Her blindsided brain finally recognised it was a helicopter. Noisily, brutally drowning out the beautiful birdsong and the once calm environment. He wasn't just leaving. This was an *extraction*. There was no other word for it. A precision operation to retrieve him from this hell zone as quickly as possible and return him to the soulless world in which he lived. Saving him from having to face things he'd once loved. Things that hurt.

But she was the one hurt. So very hurt. 'You're leaving right *now*?'

'It's the right thing to do.'

'Right thing for who?'

Because he didn't want to face her reaction for too long? Suddenly she was angry. Too bad for him. She'd never complained before—never stopped her mum and asked her to stay. Never stood up to her grandmother. Never asked her grandfather for help. She'd never fought for something that she'd really wanted. She'd never told them how their actions had really made her feel.

Not. This. Time.

Not when it was Ash himself who'd pulled this strength from her. Who'd shown her. She couldn't stop the hurt and anger from bubbling out of her now.

'You thought you could get away that easily?' She stepped towards him. 'You thought I'd say nothing—just smile and wave because I'm meek and useless at standing up for what I want?'

She had been. She wasn't doing that any more.

He didn't flinch. Didn't smile. He looked as angry as she felt. 'What do you want?'

'More,' she said bluntly. 'And I think you do too. But you're afraid. You got spooked yesterday. Because you talked to me and now you're worried...'

He stilled. The helicopter had landed, the pilot cutting the engine so there was a fading whine.

'What am I worried about?' he asked harshly.

'You want to stay like this for ever, don't you?'

'Like what?'

'Angry. Denying yourself or anyone else in your life anything more.'

'I'm not—'

'You're *so* angry. Because you're hurt. And scared.

You think you're running away because you don't want to deal with *my* emotions, but it's your own emotions you're really running away from.'

She'd gone too far. But it felt good—exhilarating even. She couldn't silently let him leave.

'What emotions do you think they are?'

'That you love it here. That you've had a better time with me than you expected. That maybe…' It seemed brazen to even think it and she couldn't *quite* voice it. 'You swim endless lengths to nowhere to avoid what's right here in front of you.'

'*You're* right in front of me, Merle.'

Her heart pounded in her throat. 'Exactly.'

He stared at her. 'You've been the perfect distraction.'

And that was all she'd been? *No*.

'I told you right from the start that I could never be anything to anyone,' he argued. 'Certainly not to someone like you, Merle.'

'Someone like me?'

'Someone who deserves *more*—'

'We *all* deserve more,' she snapped. 'Everyone deserves to love and be loved. People only seem to become less deserving when they've had that love lacking in their life too long. When they *think* they don't deserve it. Then they start to act in ways that ensure they don't get it.'

That was him. Cutting things short.

'We want different things, Merle. You know there's no point drawing this out.'

'Different things?' She took another step nearer to him. 'You never want to find love? Never have a family?'

She didn't know why she asked. He'd already said he'd never marry and, given his scrupulous attention to avoiding an accidental pregnancy, she knew he didn't want to be his father with secret children everywhere. But worst case for Ash wasn't just an accidental pregnancy but *any* pregnancy at all. He'd never want children. But Merle did. To build her own family and ensure they had everything she'd missed out on.

'If I stay now, you'll only be more hurt,' he said brutally. 'You don't have to stay to finish the job.'

The breath was sucked from her. 'Of course I do,' she said heatedly. 'I need this job.'

'I'll pay—'

'I don't want your money!' she yelled at him, furious that he'd reduced this to a transactional debate.

He didn't look repentant. In fact, anger mottled his skin. 'You know I didn't mean it like that.'

'There's no other meaning to it. What exactly would you be paying me for?'

He clenched his teeth. 'Merle—'

'Ask *me* for more, Ash.' She'd lost it and now her most desperate wish poured out. 'Ask me for *all* my firsts.'

An endless second of silence followed. He looked shell-shocked. And as he shook his head, he barely breathed. 'I never should have—'

'Don't even start with that. Don't pretend it meant more to me than it did to you.' She sizzled with sudden certainty. 'You want more too but it terrifies you,' she said. 'That's why you're running away. But too bad, Ash. Because here it is and you have to listen anyway. I want more. I want you. I want everything from you.

With you.' She clutched the back of the nearest deck-chair to stop herself from shaking. 'I want your first *I love you.*' Her deepest wish broke free. Because she was damned certain he'd never said that to anyone. '*That* should be *mine.*' She drew a fierce breath. 'And you want to know why? Because I love you, Ash. I've totally fallen for you.'

'Merle…'

The sorrowful but bitter rejection in his eyes stilled her. In an awful moment she realised just what she'd blurted out. There was no hiding. A horrible heat of humiliation swept up and smothered her. She was that naive fool all over again, believing that someone like him could ever be interested in her. Her anger seeped out because she'd taken a risk and lost. Because she'd humiliated herself. Because, despite that fact, she couldn't believe that he didn't feel this the way she did.

'Don't let him win, Ash,' she muttered. 'If you stay isolated? Never finding someone the way you should? Never having happiness and security? Never being loved and loving? That's letting your father win.'

'Merle…'

In the way he said her name she heard it all. The regret. The refusal. The *rejection.*

'*You* told me to be honest,' she chastised him bitterly.

Yet even though she hated this, *she* couldn't regret the difference within her. She didn't want to return to reticent, invisible Merle. She wanted to stay bold, stay ready to get stuck into life and love. Stay strong enough to make these stupid mistakes. Because maybe one day it wouldn't be a mistake. She'd just wanted that day to be *today.* She wanted Ash.

'You're a romantic,' he dismissed her. 'And I'm an idiot for ever thinking you could handle this. I'm sorry.'

No. She rejected his assessment. She was *not* Rose. She wasn't hoping—imagining—there was more to this than there really was. She'd seen it in his eyes. She'd felt it in his body as he'd moved in hers. And she was *not* letting him tell her otherwise.

'You might deny your own feelings, but you don't get to tell me *my* feelings aren't real,' she said. 'This is special. What we have could be amazing. It is amazing.' They were more than lovers. They were a match.

'I have to leave.'

There was a pilot in that helicopter who could probably see her desperation in this pathetic scene in front of him, but Merle didn't care.

'You can't. We're still talking—'

'There's nothing more to say. There's nothing here for me any more.'

Even though she didn't believe him, she could see how badly *he* wanted to believe it. How badly he was fighting against listening to her. Fighting the tension within himself. It wasn't easy. Which was why he'd arranged such an immediate escape. A quick goodbye because he was a coward. Because he wasn't sure he could complete it?

Now he wouldn't even look her in the eyes.

'You told me I was too focused on seeing the good in people, that I didn't want to consider how they'd treated me. That I avoided seeing that truth. But no one is as good at avoiding things as you are,' she said angrily. 'Why not face the problems, Ash? Why not try to fix them? Instead of hiding for ever and letting them grow so big they consume you? If you always run away, you'll never find peace.'

Or love.

The waves of hurt kept coming as he didn't acknowledge her words. He just moved, picking up the small leather carry-all from the deck and stepping away. It was shockingly, unnecessarily sudden.

'You're the one who can't handle this,' she said. 'You're the one eternally isolated by fear.'

His shoulders stiffened. 'I have to go.'

'Kiss me goodbye, then, Ash.' She hurled the challenge at him. 'I *dare* you.'

His face paled, his jaw clamped—highlighting even more his spectacular angular cheekbones. Sharp, and angry, and barely controlled.

Silence screamed between them. She held his gaze as he stepped nearer. But the flare in his eyes gave him away. Or at least she hoped it did. Angry as she was with him, she needed him to know *her* truth. This wasn't a plea for him to stay any more. It was a pure expression of her own emotion.

I love you.

The press of his mouth on hers was hard, his lips compressed. Merle arched her neck, taking the almost bruising weight and then pushed back—with a softening of her own lips, with the slide of her tongue. She heard a choked sound in the back of his throat as he relented and released his hold on himself. And she stole in—all loving, passionate strokes. Warmth flowed, relief flooded in. Touching him like this? Feeling his rising response? Her heart soared. Love in a kiss. Love in a wordless, honest gift—

That he suddenly tore free from. He stared down at her, his breathing heavy. But he said nothing.

Reality slammed into her. She was never going to see him again. And she was angry with him for making her think even for a moment that she could have had more. That she could even dare *ask* for more. She went back to gripping the back of the damned deckchair. For support. To stop herself from following him and crying. From throwing herself in front of that damned helicopter in lovelorn desperation. To squeeze tightly to ride through the wave of pain as he turned and strode across that perfect tennis court that he despised.

They could've been more. They could have had more. They could have had everything that mattered. He couldn't see that. He completely disagreed.

Which had to mean that she'd been wrong.

CHAPTER TWELVE

Ash STRIVED TO stay busy, setting himself a hellfire week of work. He read reports, organised face-to-face meetings, inspected new prospects. But whenever he thought he'd found the sweet relief of pure focus, an image flashed into his mind—a shot of her in the pool, the gleam in her eye at a mid-play move of a board game, a portrait of her smile. Stills that switched the rest of the world off, meaning he could see only that moment, feel again the ripple of pleasure...only to suffer a tearing ache the milli-second he realised it was a mere mirage. His sadistic mind spasmodically tortured him with emotion-drenched memories that were too deep and good to be real. And he couldn't shut it off.

By midweek, he'd decided he'd reflect. Maybe if he remembered it all, if he methodically thought over every interaction, of every day, he could then compartmentalise it into his mental history box and move forward. But remembering made his skin burn hot and then goosebump. It made that tearing ache in his chest rip even wider. It made his breathing uneven and restlessness surge. He closed his eyes and willed for some perspective.

He wasn't missing *her*.

Maybe he could class it as a warped holiday romance? That—particularly given the location—he'd succumbed to a complicated set of sensations. He'd sought physical escape from the horrible recollections and unhappiness of discovering how fundamentally the property had been changed…and the switch from misery to delight had been so intense he'd attributed more meaning to the pleasure he'd felt with her. The problem with that classification was the disservice to Merle. *She* was much more than a distraction. She was much more than someone he'd had good sex with. She was more than a moment in time.

By the end of the week he'd realised that yes, he missed *her*. With every breath, every beat of his heart, he ached with loss. Beneath that, a feral anger prowled deep, growing exponentially bigger. She didn't contact him. He didn't contact her. It had to be finished. It was for her benefit. And this misery he felt now, he deserved. Because she deserved more than him—in every way.

He hated who he was. Not good enough. Not committed enough. He would inevitably let her down. Better now than in the future though, when it would only be worse.

But her words—that declaration—tormented him.

Ask me for all my firsts…

On the Saturday following his return to Sydney, Ash arranged a brief meeting with his half-brother. There were issues that had been outstanding for too long, and somehow catching up with him felt more important than it ever had.

Leo was impeccably on time, of course. His starched white shirt hurt Ash's jaded, sleep-deprived eyes. His half-brother was a half-inch shorter, neater and more legitimate-looking with his short hair and sharply fitted suit. So incredibly serious. There was only a glimmer of a smile in his eyes as he joined Ash at the waterfront cafe for a coffee. It had been a few weeks since they'd last caught up. Their interactions were mostly via messages, and mostly they only discussed heavy decisions regarding the business.

'You've been keeping well?' Leo's eyes narrowed as he glanced at Ash and took the seat alongside him.

The fact Leo had asked meant Ash knew he must look like death.

'Yeah. Fine.' Ash coughed the rasp from his throat and moved straight to business. 'Thanks for arranging the archival work on Waiheke.'

Leo studied him impassively. 'Have you considered the options for the property?'

Yes. Decisions needed to be made. It wasn't fair on either of his half-siblings to drag out the process any longer. They'd already divided the proceeds from the other personal properties three ways. 'I can't sell that one. If you and Grace agree, I'd like to buy you out.'

He didn't actually need their consent—the house was his. But he wanted to do right by them.

'You want to keep the beach house in New Zealand?' Leo didn't look surprised. 'Fine by me.'

Ash breathed out. He already knew Grace wouldn't object. She'd been so appalled to discover her true lineage last year that she'd said she didn't want anything from the estate at all. Ash didn't blame her for that anger. But he refused to let her give up all of her claim. He'd transfer her share to her—what she then did with it was her choice.

As for the beach house? Selling it no longer seemed right. Merle's assessment had hit a nerve. It shouldn't be the preserve of one wealthy family—a paradise that only a few privileged people got to enjoy. Somehow he'd work out some way to restore some soul to it.

'Are you sure you want to stay on at the company?' he asked Leo.

He'd been astounded that Leo had stepped in to take over as CEO after their father's death. When he considered that Hugh had refused to acknowledge Leo even after the DNA test had proven his paternity, the fact Leo had wanted to turn around the sliding fortunes of the company was impressive. Ash wouldn't have been bothered to see the business fail. But the business supported so many *other* people…there was the rub. Leo had an intense sense of responsibility and honour that Ash respected. Though the fact that Leo had defiantly taken the Castle name while Hugh was alive enough to be apoplectic about it still made Ash smile.

Now Leo nodded. 'I'm enjoying the challenge.'

Leo generally looked so serious; Ash wondered if he ever really enjoyed anything.

'You have my full support, you know that, right?' Ash grimaced. 'If you ever need me to do something.'

'I know.' Leo sipped his coffee. Drinking strong coffee was a habit they shared. 'You're busy with your own empire though.'

'That hasn't stopped you managing two.'

Leo shot him some serious side-eye. 'But I don't have a social life or any other…distractions.'

Ash smiled and shook his head. Leo was a workaholic machine with no balance at all.

'They're not distractions.' Ash tried to assume a semblance of his usual attitude. 'They're like mini-breaks. For medicinal purposes. All work and no play…'

But Ash didn't believe his own words. He didn't feel like having a social life ever again. Apparently he'd been cured of the penchant for frivolous one-night bursts of fun.

A frown furrowed Leo's brow as he contemplated the depths of his coffee. 'Actually…' Leo suddenly glanced at Ash. 'There's a charity event at Kingston Towers tonight. Half of Sydney society is going to be there.'

'Your ideal market,' Ash noted.

'But not my ideal night.' Leo took a mouthful of coffee before releasing a sharp breath. 'You don't want to show up and help take the heat off me?'

Ash mirrored his half-brother and sipped the scalding black coffee to avoid speaking immediately. It was the first time Leo had asked him for anything, and it would be the first time in years that Ash showed up at a Castle Holdings event. It would be—in society and business pages—a notable occurrence.

His first impulse was to decline. Not because it was his father's company—he saw it as Leo's now. But because he'd felt a physical rejection inside at the thought of socialising. But he *should* accept. Maybe if he returned to his usual lifestyle, he'd feel better sooner. Maybe he'd made a mistake this week by staying isolated in his penthouse and at work. Maybe he needed to get back on the party horse…

That tearing ache in his chest widened. He finally recognised it as emptiness. And he knew speaking sassy nothings with a series of society babes on the never-ending party circuit wasn't going to fill the void. But there was another reason, a far more important reason, to say *yes*.

He'd lived most of his life without knowledge of either of his half-siblings. Now he knew about them and, while Grace preferred not to engage, Leo was here. Maybe the two of them could make something more from the little they had between them? Ash could show up for Leo.

'Sure,' he said firmly. 'What time should I arrive?'

Ash had regrets the moment he walked into the gorgeously decorated ballroom. The usual were present—the old money, the newly famous, the current influencers, the prettiest, the most 'interesting'… Phones and cameras were everywhere—capturing the stunning set-up, glamorous make-up, fantastic food. Ash wasn't hungry for any of it. But he could fake it with the best of them.

He had, he realised, been faking it for a long time now. Finally he realised everything he'd pushed so deep down for so long had floated back to the surface. And he had to face it. More than anything, he had to face what Merle had said to him. What she'd opened up in him. What she'd made him *feel*.

A sense of urgency swept over him.
He needed to go. He needed to—
Be there for Leo.

He slammed on his own brakes. He could build at least *one* better relationship in his life, couldn't he?

He chatted to a few people before deciding he needed a glass of water to clear his head. On his way to the bar he passed by a redhead. He glanced again because there was something familiar in her slightly oddly angled stance. That was when he recognised her. She looked vastly different to the awkward girl who'd come to school all those years ago. With her black skirt and silk shirt and her hair tied back from her face, now she looked capable and confident.

'Rose? What are you doing here?' he asked before thinking better of it.

But she didn't flinch or look embarrassed as he'd have expected from her. Rather her eyes widened and she actually smiled. 'Ash Castle!' she exclaimed. 'It's been ages.'

'Yeah.' He felt a little winded at her easy friendliness. Of all the people to bump into—why here and now after all this time? What *was* she doing here? 'I'm sorry about what happened back at school,' he suddenly blurted because it was right at the front of his mind. He instantly regretted it. What an idiot to bring that up in public.

Rose frowned in confusion, then he saw the penny drop. To his astonishment she actually giggled. 'Oh, you mean *that*.' She laughed again but then sobered and suddenly looked apologetic. 'You poor thing, that must've been hell for you. Your mother was so unwell and none of us knew how bad it was.'

Um. Was she feeling sympathy for *him*?

'Yeah, but I acted…' He didn't even want to say it.

'Ash, that was *years* ago.' There was no distress in

her eyes, no embarrassment, no concern. She certainly wasn't blushing. Because she really wasn't bothered. If anything, her smile had grown bigger and more care-free. 'Have you been feeling bad all this time?'

He hesitated.

'Forget it,' she said. 'Truly.'

He'd thought he'd devastated her. That he'd blighted her life. He clearly hadn't. She barely batted an eyelash about it now. She didn't look at him with any adulation, any interest even. Just courtesy. He mocked himself bit-terly—it had been so arrogant of him to assume he'd truly hurt her. But he'd thought he'd really damaged her. The way his mother had been damaged. Had he confused the impact on Rose with the devastation his mother had felt? And his mother had so many *other* rea-sons to react so angrily, so devastatingly, to that fool-ish, selfish act. Everything had got jumbled up inside him, and he'd been so upset he'd thought of everything in extremes.

Now he'd never been so relieved to be wrong about something.

'You seem really well,' he said feebly.

'I am, thanks.' She glanced past him. 'But I'm afraid I need to get going—there's someone I really have to see.'

'Yes. Of course.'

Yeah, she wasn't interested in lingering to talk to him. She wasn't interested in him at all any more. She'd grown up and moved on. Whereas he? He'd got stuck back there—in that hot mess of guilt and betrayal and hurt. But maybe he didn't need to be there any more. Maybe he'd been an idiot.

He kept a grip on himself long enough to chat to a few more guests. From a distance he saw his half-brother shoot him an appreciative nod of the head. A few women smiled, 'available and interested' signals lighting their eyes. He smiled but kept his distance and talked up Leo's new development plans some more as, inside, feelings crystallised into hard rocks of unavoidable truth.

Suddenly he couldn't stay a second longer. He couldn't find Leo to say goodbye. He'd send him a text tomorrow. He asked his driver to just drive. He didn't want to go to his empty penthouse, didn't want to stay at the party, didn't want to take up any of the offers he'd had.

Instead, he took the back seat and closed his eyes, partially soothed by the low hum of the powerful engine and the constant movement. That sensation of escape was essential. But what he was struggling with was stuck inside him. There was no escape from that.

He'd been wrong. Seeing Rose had made him reassess the fallout of those actions of so long ago. Leo was bold and in control. Grace happily doing her thing in Melbourne. Rose was clearly confident and in control of her life. Apparently the only person still bogged down in all that horror was him—stuck in resentment and isolation and self-loathing. Stuck so he couldn't get out to where he wanted—and needed—to be.

Merle Jordan didn't like good-looking or popular guys. She didn't trust *anyone's* motivations. Ash didn't blame her. She'd judged him, and that long-burning rebelliousness in Ash had meant he'd encouraged her to. He'd made it so easy for her—playing up to that image.

He'd been everything she'd been wary of. But then, with that perfect eyesight of hers, she'd seen through him. She'd seen more in him than *he'd* wanted to believe was there. She'd seen right from the start that he was hiding.

Of course he was hiding—he'd been hiding, faking, for years. Just as his father had. No matter that the lies were *different*, he was still living a lie. Still using a facade to hide behind. He'd hated who he was beneath it. And now he hated that he couldn't be the guy she needed. The last thing he'd wanted to do was hurt her, but he had. Badly. He'd hurt himself too. The cavernous hopelessness had become a physical pain. She deserved so much better than what he'd offered. Than what he *was*. Or what he'd *thought* he was. Because maybe he'd taken it all too far?

For so long he'd thought he was just like his father. For so long he'd tried not to be but felt that hopelessness deep inside. That there was something within him that he couldn't escape. That he was someone who'd hurt the people he loved the most. But that wasn't entirely true, was it? Because he hadn't hurt Rose the way he'd thought. Or maybe he had, but she'd long forgiven and forgotten and moved on to better things. Because people failed and people made mistakes but they tried again. Ash wasn't used to failure in a business sense. He didn't have much experience of trying again. But couldn't he? Couldn't *he* be better?

Because the person he'd hurt recently? She was the one who mattered most. Her words—the ones he'd tried not to listen to—rang in his ears like town hall bells pealing through the county.

Don't let him win.

Was that what he was doing? Wasn't she right? Wouldn't having a committed, happy, *honest* relationship be the ultimate act of rebellion against his father's memory? Even when facing the worst, Merle had hope and strength. She wanted more for him. But also for herself. Because she could admit how she felt. She had courage. He wanted to be better for her—brave like her. And he didn't give a damn about his bloody father any more.

He didn't want Merle to be alone, and the last thing he wanted was for her to find someone else. In time, she would. She was too beautiful, too loveable not to. Suddenly his old arrogance soared inside. No one else— *no one*—could give her what he could give her. He wanted her to have everything she'd missed out on. Not material wealth or luxury. It was simpler than that. Scarier. But how did he create a bond that would only strengthen them? How did he reach out to her? How did he do *any* of this? For all of his supposed intelligence, he was absolutely clueless.

It felt as if that empty ache inside was filling with his own blood.

I want your first I love you.

That plea had devastated him. But she didn't realise she'd already had some of his firsts. Things he'd never told anyone. Things he'd never done before. Spending that time with her. Laughing like that with her. *Playing* in a way that was more than superficial, in a way that formed serious foundations.

But she didn't know, because he'd not told her. Because he'd been a coward. It turned out he was better than Merle Jordan—the hide-away queen herself—

at avoidance. He finally accepted that he'd run away not to 'protect her' from him. He'd been protecting himself. Because he didn't want that pain of loss. Because he didn't want to be rejected. Because he didn't want to be a disappointment. So he'd got in first. Everything that terrified him, he'd done to her. He was a jerk.

And now he felt terrible for it. The biggest mistake of his life had left him balancing on the narrowest ledge of a cliff. He didn't have long to stop himself falling. Merle Jordan was like a sprite. She'd lit his life for only a short time, but he'd not appreciated her true value. So he'd left her. He'd lost her. He couldn't lose her for ever. He couldn't let her disappear, never to be found again. So how did he reach out? How did he try to make this better? How did he fix what he'd broken?

With the truth.

CHAPTER THIRTEEN

MERLE WAS SICK of being stuck in a mega-mansion all by herself riding the roller coaster of heartbreak and hope. She'd spent the week storming through the boxes in silence, determined to still do a good job. But determined to do a *fast* job. The sooner she was done, the sooner she could escape, and the sooner she could recover. Because the hope side of the equation was slipping.

A couple of days after Ash's abrupt departure a load of groceries had been delivered. A mass of fresh fruit and vegetables, meat and fish and, yes, even more instant noodles. She hated that he'd been that thoughtful when he'd refused to care. Was it only pity? With a sprinkle of guilt perhaps. Either way, it was a scattering of emotional crumbs she really didn't want from him. Because she wanted *everything*. Instead, Ash Castle had left her with only ash—the remnants of her pride, of her memories of that last week, with her burned heart.

She'd worked through the whole week, then the weekend. She had that week off with Ash to make up for anyway. She'd focused on cataloguing one item after another, not letting her gaze wander to the pool outside, not letting her mind wander to wisps of conversation, to the echo of laugher and sweet sighs. And she was never, *ever*, thinking of that last kiss—where she'd tried to pour her soul into him. To show him what she felt in the hope he wouldn't have been able to hold back. But he had.

She'd half-hoped to find something of his mother's, knowing it would mean so much to him. But there was nothing. There wouldn't be even that littlest of happy endings.

She needed a break now. She needed to restore some balance to herself. She'd avoided the places they'd been together. Most especially the pool. But it was a stunningly hot day and she refused to deny herself the simple pleasure of a dip. She refused to let the heartache stop her. She was brave. She could handle it, couldn't she?

Ash couldn't remember feeling anxiety like this. His hands felt damp, his pulse raced, skipping unpredictably. The helicopter couldn't fly fast enough. Yet, as it descended towards the grassy helipad at the far end of the tennis court, he suddenly wanted time to slow. He wanted a chance to think through his plan once more. But there wasn't time. Nor was there any real plan.

There was no way she could've failed to hear his arrival. Unless, of course, she'd already left the property. His heart pounded even more irregularly. He walked towards the house and the helicopter lifted away behind him. As its noise faded he heard another—a splash. He moved more quickly to be sure, but there she was. In the pool. His nymph, swimming as if she hadn't a care in the world. But as he walked nearer he saw her eyes, and the expression in them smote his heart. She was pale and her fine features drawn, but she'd never looked more beautiful. She held her head high as she climbed the ladder and reached for a towel, hiding from him.

'You're still here.' His voice sounded croaky. The paper bag he carried felt both too small and too heavy.

'I told you I'd stay.'

'I wouldn't have blamed you if you'd left,' he said. 'Most people would've already.'

'I had a job to do.'

Was the only reason she'd stayed because she was contractually obligated? Because she needed the money? Or was it because she'd made the commitment and Merle saw her commitments through—even to people who'd hurt her? That was what she'd done for her family, wasn't it? She'd done what was right.

'Why are you here?' she suddenly asked. 'You were never coming back.'

'I needed to see you. I have something I wanted to give to you.'

She stiffened. 'You don't need to give me anything just because you feel guilty about…whatever.'

'Merle—'

'You didn't need to come back here and try to make… I don't need this from you.'

'Please, Merle.' He held it out to her.

It wasn't even wrapped properly. She pulled the small volume out of the brown paper bag and when she read the cover her eyes widened and her colour leeched, leaving her looking ghostly.

It wasn't some pretty edition like she ought to have. It was a mass-produced paperback that cost only a few dollars. He'd wanted to gift her something meaningful. That she would treasure not because of its financial value, but for the thought behind it. He wanted—hoped—she would understand. 'I found it at the airport on the way,' he muttered apologetically. 'I thought about a rare edition, hoped for a hardback even, but there wasn't time.'

He'd been desperate to get to her once he'd realised what a damned fool he'd been.

A touch of pink stole into her cheeks, combatting her pallor. 'This is better,' she said. 'Ordinary things can be loved too.'

'But I bent the spine when I wrote in it,' he added, even more apologetically.

'You wrote in it?' Her gaze flashed back to him.

A tiny bubble of hope formed in that cavernous ache in his chest when he saw the intensity in her expression. He hid his tense fists in his trouser pockets and resisted the burning urge to drag her against him. He'd never felt such uncertainty. But if he knew Merle at all, he knew she would appreciate this.

Now there was a rosy depth to her cheeks. Now her beautiful brown eyes were gazing right into his and he couldn't look away from them. He couldn't help but hope that he was really seeing what he so badly wanted in those eyes.

'The ink is archival quality, apparently,' he mumbled helplessly. 'So it'll last. It won't fade. Even if you put it in the sun.'

But she didn't open the cover to read what he'd written. She didn't even look down at it. Her gaze was fixed on him and suddenly he felt too exposed. Too raw.

'Ash Castle,' she murmured softly and stepped closer, 'are you blushing?'

More than that—his hands were shaking and he felt hot and cold all over. He really didn't like the vulnerability. 'Just read it,' he said. 'Tell me you love it.'

Tell me you love me.

He wanted to hear that again. He was desperate to record it and keep it so he could replay it over and over. His pulse hammered. But she still didn't look at the book. She held it out to him.

'You read it to me,' she said quietly.

He stared at her. He saw wariness still in those beautiful eyes, but he saw hope too. The shy desire for so much more. His throat was unbearably tight. He didn't need to take the book that she held in visibly trembling fingers. And it was her trembling that tore him apart. Her trembling that showed how much this mattered to her. It mattered to him too. So impossibly much.

'"For my beautiful Merle."' He paused to cough away the huskiness, but it didn't work. He didn't think he could get to the end of it. But he had to try. '"Because precious things matter. Because you're my treasure. Because I want you to have all my firsts that truly matter and everything else I have to give. Because I love you and I will for ever and for always. Ash."'

Merle couldn't move, couldn't breathe past the massive lump of emotion weighing her down. 'That's why you came back?' she whispered.

'For you. Yes.' A storm of emotion swirled in his eyes. A world of promise. 'Because it's awful without you. Because I've been such an idiot. But mostly because I'm in love with you and I can't stand to be apart from you any longer.'

He'd just said it again. The words she'd wanted so much. The ones that meant the world.

She clutched the book to her chest. It was so simple, so perfect, and what it symbolised was so precious. He'd listened. He'd understood. And he cared.

'Merle...' His voice dropped.

Goose pimples feathered across her skin at the ache evident in his voice. Her eyes stung. He meant it. He stood so rigidly, as if he couldn't trust himself even to breathe.

He was waiting. For her.

She began to shake so badly she had to wrap her arms around her waist and tightly grip the towel and the book all together in a damp mess. All the emotion was leaking out as if her body were a sieve. And as it did, it exposed a hard knot of agony deep in her chest. The knot that had formed when he'd rejected her, when he'd walked out and left her alone. And now it was impossible to move.

'Merle?' That old smile bubbled up into his eyes— a hint of his tease. 'One last chance?'

Taking a step seemed impossible, but that knot loosened and she moved. He met her halfway and his arms were around her and his heat and strength warmed where she'd been so cold.

'I'm sorry,' he mumbled against her hair. 'I've been such a fool. I thought I was broken. I thought I wasn't worthy. But I want to try. I want to be better for you.'

That tight, hard knot unravelled. Tears spilled as he pressed her so close that she felt his racing heart as it pounded against her breast. The tremors in his muscles matched hers and that disbelieving desperation made her cling to him.

And he held her. 'You were right. So right. I've been hiding. I went to see Leo. And I saw Rose.'

She stilled, listening intently, her heart clogging her throat.

'She was fine, Merle. So's Leo. Seeing them both made me realise that I might've been wrong about the fallout from what had happened back then. And if I'd been wrong about that, then I was likely wrong about other things too. Most importantly, I've never felt this way about anyone other than you. And I can love and I can commit and I want everything. *With you*,' he added, his hands roving, pressing her closer. 'I missed you.'

Her eyes closed and she melted, tucking her face into the warmth of his neck, breathing in his scent, his nearness. Finally believing this was real.

'I don't want anything else. Not anyone, anything,' he growled. 'I just want you. With me. All the time. Okay?'

Someone wanted her. Not just someone. *Ash*.

She wasn't some distraction from this house, not some project to assuage old guilt. She wasn't some mere affair either. She was his *treasure*. As he was hers.

'Sweetheart?' He slid his hands in her hair and tilted her head.

Merle lifted her chin and he met her halfway. The kiss was more than scorching, it was acute—almost agonising—perfection and it melted the remnants of that knot inside and allowed the most precious of all of her feelings to flow freely towards him.

'I love you, Ash.'

His breath shuddered. This time he didn't ignore her. This time he answered with touch, with heat and infinite care. It was as if his sole purpose was to give her pleasure, to show her how passionately he felt about her. How much he'd missed her. How much he needed her. How much he loved her.

He loved her and loved her and loved her.

She felt it in every kiss, every touch. She responded—unable to restrain anything, and she didn't want to. She caressed him and the ache and emptiness that had been a constant these last few days dissolved. She needed to share and show her feelings for him. She shuddered as he peeled away her swimsuit. He stroked her tenderly, his hands shaking as badly as hers were. They stumbled together until he took some semblance of control and tumbled her down onto one of the sun-loungers.

'It's too sunny out here,' he said.

She smiled tremulously. 'Then we'll be quick.'

He half laughed and, to her eternal relief, obliged. She just needed him *with* her.

His groan of pure joy when he pushed home was magical to her ears but she could only moan in return and lift her mouth to kiss him once more. They moved together, slick and desperate, and it was so joyous she cried again.

'I love you,' he whispered, kissed, vowed as he held her closer, pushing faster and fiercer.

Her head arched back as the sensations overwhelmed her—he was really here, loving her hot and hard, making her world shatter. And holding her still. Holding her through it all.

* * *

Eventually, she snuggled against his chest, loving the firm weight of his arm around her, holding her to him. She rested her chin on his ribs to steal a glance at his face. He looked back at her, so much more relaxed, so handsome. That old arrogance tinged his smile but there was an unguarded openness that was new.

'You were right,' he said softly. 'I've been avoiding real intimacy for years. But you got to me, Merle, and I couldn't handle it. I still…' He gazed at her so intently. 'I don't want to let you down.'

'Ash, I love *you*.'

The kiss was the sweetest, the hottest of her life and she didn't want it ever to end. He seemed to sense it, his arms tightening around her.

'It's okay, sweetheart,' he promised. 'I'm not going anywhere. I'm going to work here while you're finishing the archiving,' he murmured. 'I'll have to go to Sydney occasionally for meetings. Will you come with me?'

'You want me to?'

'I don't want to be away from you. Not for long, anyway.'

He wanted her front and centre in his life. Not hidden in the wings. Not with him under sufferance. Not unseen.

'Would you like that?' he asked after a moment. 'Your choice, Merle. I want you to have and do what you want.'

She smiled at him even as tears sprang forth all over again. 'I'd like that very much.'

They were cuddled close on the deck and Merle followed the direction of his gaze, up to the house. 'I'm sorry I didn't find anything of your mother's.'

'But you did.' He kissed her gently. 'You found the games. They brought us together.'

Her heart lifted as she saw the warmth and acceptance in his eyes. So they had.

'Are you still going to sell the house?' she asked.

Beneath her cheek his chest rose as he drew in a difficult breath. 'Actually, I was thinking you were right about it being a shame that more people don't get to come here and enjoy it. I thought we could offer it as a holiday home for cardiac patients and their families. For during their recovery or as an escape or something...' He cleared his throat. 'There might be a charity that could help us arrange that. If there isn't, we can establish one.' He paused. 'What do you think?'

She sat up to lean over him and look directly into his beautiful eyes, seeing the flash of vulnerability there. 'I think that sounds amazing. I think *you're* amazing.'

That smile broke across his face. 'Shall we go for a swim, sweetheart? And then maybe play another round of snakes and ladders?'

A bubble of pure happiness fizzed from deep within her, culminating in a satisfied giggle. That simple invitation was the most special of her life. She was with him now—included—and together they made laughter and love.

Ash Castle had opened up in the most gorgeous way and given her everything she ever could have dreamed of.

'That'll be just perfect.'

CHAPTER FOURTEEN

One year later

MERLE DECIDED THIS summer on Waiheke Island was particularly stunning. Every day had been highlighted by a brilliant sun, cloudless bright skies and views of that calm, endless sea. Today her floaty fabric jump-suit was vibrant and cool. She loved the silky feel of it as Ash firmly gripped her hand and led her down the balcony stairs.

'What are you doing?' She giggled at his determined pace. 'Where are you taking me in such a rush?'

'To my secret underground lair.' He glanced back with a suggestive waggle of his eyebrows. 'Where else?'

'The bunker?' She'd not been down there in ages. Most of the time she forgot it even existed. 'Why?'

He didn't answer. There was just another playfully suggestive smile.

They were almost a week into their month-long holiday here. They'd made Ash's old bedroom their suite, mostly so they could indulge in a decadent bubble bath most nights. During the days they pitted wits over the selection of board games. They'd taken their favourite, most precious ones back to their home in Sydney, but they'd bolstered the collection here so that the families who stayed could enjoy them. His idea of a respite holiday home had been embraced and now the house was used every weekend, even through the heart of winter.

They swiftly descended the steep stairs down into the bunker. Merle looked around, taking in the changes that had occurred since the first time she'd been in here. Ash had obviously been down here earlier because on the counter there was a bottle of champagne on ice and a selection of fresh cut fruit on a platter, together with her favourite crackers.

'What have you planned?' She shot him a laughing glance.

He paused, his head cocked at a distinct rumbling sound. 'I think the hatch just closed. I'm afraid we're locked in. Oh! No!'

Amused at his theatrical 'distress', she rose on her toes and leaned towards him. 'Are we, now?'

'Mmm. Maybe we can find a way out. I think... Is that a clue?' He peered in exaggerated fashion at the fruit platter.

She looked and saw there was something scratched on the edge of the plate. Numbers.

'Oh, yes!' She turned back to face him in mock-amazement. 'I think it might be.'

Merle knew the bunker was often used by the children who came to stay. Ash had contracted a games designer to work out an 'escape room' challenge for the guests to enjoy as part of their holiday. It was a thoughtful touch that had melted Merle's heart when he'd run it past her, but she'd not given the challenge a go herself yet. But according to the messages left in the guest book in the main house, it was one of the most popular activities.

'But this isn't fair if you know the answers to the challenges.' She laughed as he handed her a glass of champagne.

'But I *don't* know them.' He winked. 'We'll have to work it out together.'

A series of challenges took them through the bunker—one puzzle led to another, from the living area, to the kitchen, to the corridor... Working out an anagram gave them a code to unlock the bedroom at the end, and once they had made it in there they found a tiny key. Merle was entranced and fascinated, and realised that, indeed, Ash had no clue about most of the answers. It fired up the competitive nature that he'd brought out in her. She was delighted to be the one to discover a small projector that made a hologram appear. It gave them another clue to search one of the storage cupboards. When that finally unlocked, it revealed a miniature treasure chest inside.

'Do you think the key will fit?' Ash waggled his brows.

'I wonder,' she joked.

'I guess the code from the hatch will be inside,' he muttered.

Merle unlocked the little chest and lifted the lid. Then stilled.

There was no code. No next clue. There was a midnight-blue velvet cushion and carefully placed on it was a stunning solitaire.

'Merle?'

There was no denying what kind of ring that was.

Her eyes were instantly watering but she glanced up at him anyway. She couldn't not. He compelled everything from her. *'Ash.'*

He was wickedly gorgeous and that smile—the one that melted her—now spread across his face. He knew her answer already, just as she knew the question. She loved his playfulness. She loved his effort. She loved *him*.

But he spoke so seriously. 'I love you. Please will you marry me, Merle?'

Even though he knew her answer already, she heard the rough edge of vulnerability. Emotion, *truth*, throbbed. She knew that for him, too, nothing else mattered.

'Yes,' she answered swiftly and simply as tears warred with her smiles. 'There's nothing I'd like more.'

He lifted the ring from the treasure chest.

'It's beautiful,' she whispered.

Relief lit his eyes. 'There's a code in the engraving.'

'Meaning?'

'You'll have to work it out.' Holding it carefully, he angled it so she saw the stunning, intricate pattern engraved along the band and a small black stone set right inside it.

'It has a secret stone in there?' She was amazed.

'An ash-coloured diamond.' He glanced at her a little sheepishly. 'My heart.'

It was both traditional and modern, serious and playful with a hidden heart—his. Of course there was. Because Ash knew her love for symbolism, for tying memory and emotion to little treasures. So he'd made sure this ring had it all for her.

'Do you like it?'

'It's such a precious thing,' she breathed. 'You've put so much thought into it. It's *perfect,* Ash.'

So unique, so *intentional*. She adored it, but most of all she adored him. She held out her hand urgently, half-laughing as she saw how her fingers trembled. He slid the ring home.

'I'm never taking it off,' she vowed.

His smile flashed and he tugged on her hand to pull her against his body. 'What if we take everything else off?'

'Yes, please.' She could say nothing but yes to Ash Castle.

He helped her out of her pink jumpsuit, chuckling at the emerald bikini beneath it. Colour was now Merle's friend. She loved exploring all kinds of combinations, all kinds of everything, with Ash alongside her for the ride. And now, as she gazed into his eyes, her heart burst, overflowing at the hope and love she saw. In his delight at their future together. They'd both finally found love. For ever.

* * * * *

If you were blown away by
Stranded for One Scandalous Week
*you're sure to get swept up in the next instalment
of the Rebels, Brothers, Billionaires duet.*

*And don't forget to check out these other stories
by Natalie Anderson!*

The Innocent's Emergency Wedding
The Greek's One-Night Heir
Shy Queen in the Royal Spotlight
Secrets Made in Paradise
The Queen's Impossible Boss

All available now